MAVIS PERKINS
FLYING JOURNALIST

CINDY WEIGAND

To women pilots everywhere

*From a woman's first ascent in a balloon in the late 1700s,
you have flown every type of aircraft since.*

You are amazing.

ISBN: 979-8-9878848-8-1

CONTENTS

"Flying has nearly killed me many times. It has never made me rich. Yet, from the challenge of the skies, I have reached humanity's most treasured reward—life in its fullest meaning for myself and in relation to others."

— Ruth Nichols, Aviator
International Women's Aviation Hall of Fame

CHAPTER 1
OFF TO THE CIRCUS

September 1925, Long Island, New York

AERIAL GROUP THRILLS 10 THOUSAND. I had
seen headlines such as these many times during the
summer. As the owner of a newspaper, I subscribed to a
number of publications throughout the Eastern United
States and the South. The *Birmingham News* billed them as
the World's Greatest Exhibition Aviators. Not the best. The
WORLD'S GREATEST. A big claim to live up to. The
group attracted thousands of spectators, and reporters loved
to write about them. Gates seemed different than other
organizations of its type, going beyond corny stunts. Consis-
tently, articles above the crease with kickers before the body
of the article drew readers' attention. This made me wonder
if they had an actual newspaper guy working for them as a
front man.

Almost every piece featured a pilot named Jack
Ashcraft and a stuntman, Duke "Diavalo" Krantz.
According to the papers, Jack stood six feet, four inches tall
with blond hair and blue eyes. One article described him as

having a physique of "lightly packed bone and sinew." As the story goes, he hails from Texas, so reporters dubbed him "Big Jack, Cowboy Aviator."

Through the pages of their newspapers, I followed them northward—Atlanta, Baltimore, Richmond, and Washington, DC. Every article told where they would appear for their next exhibition. When I read that they were going to be in Philadelphia and surrounding cities, I, Mavis Perkins, newspaper owner and pilot, decided to check them out. The excursion gave me an excuse to take a break from the Long Island and New York scenes. While I could have used the cross-country flying time, airports were sparse and those close to Philly would be busy, so I decided to take the train and made reservations for the weekend. I would leave Friday afternoon, attend the air show Saturday, and then return to Long Island overnight, arriving home on Sunday. I called Mother and Daddy to tell them my plans so someone would know where I was.

Since I was on an excursion outside of New York, where no one knew me, I chose to wear the linen trousers and oxfords that I wore flying. I owned two pairs of slacks made specifically for outings such as this. A simple silk blouse and a straw hat completed my outfit. I hoped wearing plain clothes would deter unwelcome advances as well. They get tiresome. It didn't work.

As I boarded the train, a man looked me up and down and winked. "I like a woman who dresses in modern attire. It tells me that she has a mind of her own. How about we get to know one another over drinks later?"

"I do have a mind of my own, so no thank you," I responded, and walked on. I later thought that he had tuned in to my tailored attire. Some considered women wearing pants gauche and unbecoming. I couldn't have cared less but had to sometimes. No one knew who I was, and I intended to stay anonymous. I wanted to be just one of the crowd on this adventure.

How I appreciated the solitude of the private compartment. I carried on my valise so I wouldn't be disturbed and settled in. Pulling a notebook and pencil from my bag, I jotted down a few notes about upcoming events and ideas for articles, but soon set pencil and paper aside to watch the scenery. I ordered dinner in so I wouldn't have to talk to anyone or rebuff more unwanted advances. However, I did venture up to the observation lounge to see the night sky and get a breath of fresh air before I turned in for the night.

The next morning, I had finished breakfast and was enjoying my morning coffee when I heard a commotion as the train slowed to a stop. People ran to look out the windows of the rail cars. I put my coffee down and joined them. Out of the corner of my eye, I saw a roaring red streak go over the train, followed by two more. The train screeched to a stop at the station, and people rushed off, pushing and shoving one another. The scene was excited chaos. I stepped outside the car to see everyone looking up.

"Look!" a young boy exclaimed. "It's airplanes!"

"There's another one," a girl cried as she pointed for her mother.

Above us, three bright red biplanes emblazoned with a star on the fuselage and under the wings dove, looped, and spiraled near the train station.

"Look, they're coming back!" someone yelled.

People shaded their eyes against the bright morning sun

as the planes made chandelle turns, then headed back toward the train station. Passengers ducked when objects rained down from the planes. A rolled-up newspaper grazed my shoulder, then fell at my feet. I picked it up and spread it out. The headline leapt out at me: *THE GATES FLYING CIRCUS COMES TO TOWN!* The article said that the pilots of the group would put on a "bally Saturday morning" to encourage readers to attend the show that afternoon. Afterwards, they would take passengers for rides. The piece also offered free tickets for an airplane ride. The tickets were placed inside the paper for seven lucky individuals. Eagerly, I thumbed through the publication. To my delight, I was one of the lucky seven.

I looked over to see a young boy looking up at me. Tears welled in his eyes. "I was going to get that paper, lady."

"Joey—" his mother cautioned.

"No, it's okay," I said to the woman, who was holding a little girl by the hand. A man stood near her who I assumed was her husband.

I looked at Joey. "My apologies," I said, and reached into my bag and got a twenty-dollar bill. I handed the money to the boy. "Please take this so your whole family can take a flight together, okay?"

Joey grinned from ear to ear.

The boy looked at his parents for permission to accept the money. "Is it okay, Mom?"

I gave his parents a look that dared them not to say no. They both nodded their approval.

The father touched the boy's shoulder. "Be sure to thank the nice lady."

Joey looked up at me, grinning from ear to ear. "Thanks, lady."

"You're welcome. Have fun."

CHAPTER 2
THE GATES FLYING CIRCUS

Labor Day 1925, Philadelphia

ANXIOUS TO GET to the airfield and take my free plane ride, I looked for a taxi. As a licensed pilot, I felt silly to be so excited about a free ride a hundred feet off the ground, yet I was. The city was packed with people. Everywhere I went, I had to wait in line—to check my bag, to get a taxi, to get to the airfield. It seemed everyone wanted to see for themselves what the Gates Flying Circus was about. Finally, a cab stopped for me.

"Where you headed, lady?" the driver asked as I settled in. "Let me guess. The airfield."

"How did you know? Is everyone in town for the aerial circus?" Progress was stop-and-go as pedestrians darted in front of the cab.

"Sure are," he answered. "The press has been advertising it for weeks. It's great business for me, let me tell you. I'll make in two days what I usually make in a month. I can probably only get you within a quarter mile of the arena. It was packed with cars and all sorts of vehicles by this time yesterday."

As he predicted, the area outside the airfield overflowed with cars, trucks, and motorcycles. They were haphazardly parked; their owners had abandoned them and were walking toward the showgrounds. I joined the throng pushing and shoving to get to the bleachers. Excited children, mostly boys, ran ahead of their parents.

Then I heard a commotion behind me.

"Here come the pilots!" a boy yelled.

I turned and saw an open truck with men in aviation helmets, goggles propped up on their foreheads, riding on the bed of the truck. Some sat, legs in tall leather riding boots dangling from the edge. Others stood. One seemed particularly tall. All waved and smiled to the people who had gathered, obviously enjoying the attention. Boys swarmed them to shake their hands and possibly get an autograph. Some tried to get on the truck. The airmen helped a few aboard and let them ride for a few minutes before dropping them off. Adults and children alike followed the vehicle until they were turned away at the gate and the pilots let through.

I had never seen such an aerial spectacle, even at Roosevelt Field on Long Island, where there was plenty of aviation-related activity. My first impression? The Gates Flying Circus was appropriately named. It was a circus. But I was interested in only one thing—meeting Big Jack.

On my way to the bleachers, I passed a canteen truck and caught a steaming whiff of cooking hamburgers and hot dogs. Squeezing into a small space on the end of a bleacher bench, I looked around and took in the scene. Where I sat was a large open grandstand for spectators. Next to it was covered seating. There were as many people standing as there were seated. A tent off to the right had a sign at the entrance that read: *Press, Pilots, and VIPs only.*

I'm glad I thought to bring my press pass, I thought.

A track had been constructed at the airfield. Five bright red biplanes like I had seen that morning were lined up outside the arena, behind the bleachers. Near them was a fuel truck with *Texaco* written on the side. Beyond the fuel truck, mechanics worked on an airplane under a tent. In the center of the infield was an ambulance. The atmosphere was electric with anticipation. The place smelled of fuel, castor oil, and human sweat. I noticed that there were now two planes lined up. The announcer—or barker, if you will —strutted out. He had red hair and wore a white shirt with the sleeves rolled up and a brown tie.

"Ladies and gentlemen! Welcome to the Philadelphia Gates Flying Circus air show!"

The crowd applauded and cheered.

"What you will witness today will be the most dazzling, the most daring, the most thrilling aerial exhibition performed by the greatest pilots in the world. They will loop, spin, spiral, and perform maneuvers that you thought were impossible. Ladies and gentlemen, I present to you the GATES FLYING CIRCUS!"

More cheering and clapping. No one noticed that three of the airplanes had taken off from the field behind the grandstand and circled for their grand entrance.

At exactly one thirty, on cue after they were announced, the planes roared low over the grandstand and infield. Spectators reveled at the sight. The three performed five simultaneous side-by-side loops, then the falling leaf maneuver. Afterwards, they separated and stunted on their own in three different parts of the sky—a real three-ring circus. One flew upside down over the heads of the spectators, causing them to duck. Later, the pilot flew upside down in front of the bleachers.

Another flew low with a rope ladder dangling from the right wing. A man in an automobile racing around the track reached for the rope as it approached the car. He caught it, waved to the crowd, and climbed up to the airplane. There he dangled for a few minutes before scrambling into the front cockpit, still waving.

The third airplane knocked over a line of empty soda bottles with the tip of its wing. This was followed by a dazzling array of aerial maneuvers. The pilot spun down, causing everyone to cover their heads and duck, then pulled out at the last instant and gained altitude. Seconds later, the pilot turned off his engine. Nonchalantly, he pulled out a bugle and played a tune before he landed and taxied off with hands raised to the cheering crowd. As the plane exited the field, I saw *Jack Ashcraft* painted on the side. Another plane took off so that three aircraft would be in the air at all times.

The pilot who had flown upside down landed and taxied in front of the crowd, then reached into the front cockpit. To everyone's surprise and delight, a German Shepherd peered out, wearing goggles. He and the pilot jumped from the wing and ran up and down in front of the audience. The announcer introduced the pilot as Clyde "Upside-Down" Pangborn and the canine as "Judge, Head of Security," and assured the crowd that he was safely secured in the cockpit.

The aerial stunting continued for several more minutes until the crowd became restless, anxious for something different. Noticing what was happening, the barker signaled to one of the pilots on the ground, who I believe was Jack. I looked at his line of sight. A tall, wiry man in white coveralls and white headband exited a tent, wiping his hands, and climbed into the front cockpit of Jack's plane while a roustabout fueled the plane. They took off. The whole process took less than two minutes.

The barker stepped into the arena. The other planes landed and exited the field. At the sight of the announcer with his megaphone, the crowd quieted down in anticipation.

"And now, ladies and gentlemen, we have a special treat for you! Our amazing daredevil! He'll risk his life so you can tell the story to your grandkids! The Gates Flying Circus presents The GREAT DIAVALO!"

On cue, a plane swooped down in front of the grandstands and bleachers and back, Diavalo on top of the wing, arms outflung. Thrilled, the spectators stood and cheered. He then lowered himself to the bottom wing, weaving his way around the struts and wires. The stuntman then dropped to the spreader bar and hung from his knees, and then by one foot. Suddenly, he dropped, saved by a cable attached to his ankle. Scrambling to the top wing, he pretended to slip. The crowd collectively caught their breath. Some covered their eyes, but I watched and thought I saw him connect a cable that was attached to a belt around his waist to the plane, then stand upright. The pilot gained altitude, then dove in preparation for a loop. The crowd went wild. As the plane sped by, I saw *Jack Ashcraft* painted on the fuselage.

For his grand finale, Diavolo straddled the back of the fuselage like a horse and rode the plane down. Until then, I hadn't noticed that there was a saddle attached to the plane. The pilot maneuvered the plane so that the movement mimicked a bucking motion to the amusement of the crowd.

As a journalist, I was accustomed to covering events of

all sorts. However, none of them had prepared me for the display that had unfolded before me. As a pilot, I imagined performing some of the stunts and wondered if I could ever be that good.

Rides started at three.

CHAPTER 3
PILOTS, PRESS, AND VIPS

WHILE OTHERS JOCKEYED in line to buy tickets for a plane ride, I headed toward the VIP tent, thinking the pilots would make an appearance there first. A glance inside the tent told me that my hunch was correct. There they were, goggles propped on top of their flight helmets, schmoozing with the press and VIPs of the town. Soot and smoke covered their cheeks and foreheads, accentuating the white around the eyes that had been protected by goggles. They looked like owls peering about.

The same guy who had announced the events stood at the opening of the tent. I flashed my press pass in his direction. He squinted to read it, but I sashayed by him before he had a chance to ask questions. The man behind the counter watched me closely. Thirsty and hot from sitting in the sun, I fanned myself. "Could I please have a glass of water?" He obliged.

"You know, lady, a classy dame like you deserves some fancy stuff," he said, and discretely handed me a tumbler of champagne. "It's on the house."

I smiled and put a couple of bucks in his tip jar. "Thank you."

Roaming around the tent, I observed with interest its occupants and caught snippets of conversation. The pilots were bantering with one another, shaking hands with people, and talking to the media. Two tall guys, one sporting a white headband and the other one wearing a flying helmet, talked to a reporter who feverishly jotted notes. A shorter guy in a dusty white shirt, a brown tie and pants, and a trilby hat listened in on the conversation. The pilot wearing the flight helmet noticed me and followed me with his eyes as I moved around the room.

"Jack, the guy asked you a question," the man in the white shirt said, pulling the pilot's attention back to the reporter.

I smiled, nodded, then disappeared into the crowd. *I definitely got his attention.*

"Red, they need you outside," someone yelled, and the fellow at the entrance took off.

I exited as well.

Outside, the circus atmosphere had intensified. The spectators had vacated the stands and were rushing toward the corrals where roustabouts were loading passengers for rides. The line was roped off and snaked around for blocks.

"We'll take you high or low, fast or slow, any way you want to go," Red exclaimed from the back of a red van with the words *WORLD'S GREATEST EXHIBITION AVIA-TORS* painted on the sides.

There was an area with barricades near a ticket booth where people paid for their tickets. A guy then ushered them to what looked like a corral, where they waited to get on a plane. There were five planes taking two to five passengers on each flight. I watched as a plane took off into the wind. The aircraft ascended into a climbing stall, belching black smoke. Meanwhile, another dropped into a turning sideslip, landed, and rolled up to the passenger corral. Simultaneously, roustabouts ushered four passengers to a ladder attached to the airplane while another assisted passengers exiting the plane on the left. Everything went off like clockwork.

Intent on getting my free ride, I looked around for someone I thought looked official. I saw the man in the dusty white shirt.

"Hello," I said. "I didn't get your name."

"Ed," he said brusquely.

"Ed, I have a ticket for a free ride. Who would I talk to about that?"

"Al. You need to talk to Al. I'll take you to him. Follow me."

Ed wove his way swiftly through the crowd to the ticket booth. I had to run to keep up with him.

"Al, this lady has a ticket for a free ride. Take care of her, will ya?" Then he disappeared into the crowd.

"Hey, Mom, there's that nice lady. Let's ride with her." I turned to see the family I'd met that morning behind me and smiled.

I turned back to Al and held out my ticket for a free ride. "Here's my free ticket. There's another twenty if I can fly by myself."

The guy smiled. "Sure thing, lady."

"Oh, and there's one last request. I want to fly with Big Jack."

The guy smiled again. "You got it."

"May I keep the ticket as a souvenir?"

"You're sure a demanding dame." He smiled and

winked. "Sure." He put an X on the ticket and handed it back to me.

Al motioned for the guy ushering people into the corral to come over. "Hey, Jim."

"Whatcha need?"

"This lovely lady wants to fly alone with Jack. She's paid extra for the privilege."

"Then she'll fly alone with Jack," Jim said, gesturing. "This way, ma'am."

At the corral, I smiled and waved the family through while I awaited my turn.

"Hey, lady, you think you're privileged?" a man said loudly.

I ignored his and other remarks, and the annoyed looks of those behind me. Jack's plane was next.

Suddenly, I heard a trumpet and looked in the direction of the sound. It was Jack. He belted out a few notes, then put away the instrument. As soon as he put his horn away, he turned off the engine and deftly sideslipped and landed. His timing was so accurate that his airplane rolled to a stop precisely at the entrance of the corral. I looked on in amazement.

"He always does that when he lands. Scares the crap out of some people," Jim said with a laugh.

"Wait here while I go talk to him. Hey, Jack!"

Listening to Jim speak, Jack looked in my direction, grinned, and winked. Jim then motioned for me to come over and gave me a hand up to the first rung of the ladder. I sensed Jack eyeing me as I lowered myself into the modified passenger seat. I looked for straps to fasten. There were none. I turned to look at Jack with my hands up, asking for an explanation.

He shrugged and grinned. "Hold on to the sides. You'll be fine."

A roustabout propped the plane, and we were off. I prepared for the first turn of my short ride. To my surprise, Jack headed out over the airfield and bleachers to open space. We flew around for fifteen minutes, and then he maneuvered back in line to land, blared out a short tune on his horn, turned off the engine, and landed.

As I exited the plane, I leaned over so he could hear me. "Thanks for the extra time, but won't you get in trouble for that?"

He looked at me with a grin, which was even more charming. "Probably, but it was worth it. It's not the first time."

I smiled. "Okay, then. Will you sign my ticket as a souvenir?" I dug a pencil out of my bag.

"Sure," he said. He signed the ticket and handed it back to me.

Someone quickly ushered me out of the landing area, and I was left watching as the planes continued to circle, land, and take off again. Passengers entered and exited the planes, happy expressions on their faces, although a few appeared airsick.

Again, their precision amazed me. I estimated that they took up to six hundred passengers that day.

Later, on the train, I relived the flight over and over. *How could such a simple, short ride be so marvelous?* I wondered, yet it had been. It was second only to the euphoria I felt after I soloed.

October 1925, Long Island, New York

THE BIG NEWS on Long Island was the 1925 National Air Races at Mitchel Field. Articles about the event filled every newspaper in Manhattan, Long Island, and the surrounding area. I needed an angle for an article. I picked up the latest issue of *Aviation*. It was devoted entirely to the upcoming event. I thumbed through it.

The list of pilots scheduled to fly was a who's who in civilian and military aviation. Doolittle, Post, Hawks, Lindbergh, Beech, and others would be there.

Page after page advertised newer and faster airplanes, high-performing engines, the best bearings and the most amazing spark plugs. Advertisers boasted innovations in various parts for planes, but what caught my eye was a simple full-page poster layout. Emblazoned at the top was:

GREETINGS!
From Trans-Continental Gates Flying Circus

of San Francisco, California
("The Daddy of them All")

The poster also stated that the exhibition team had reached New York City after five years of touring the United States from the Pacific to the Atlantic. According to the poster, on their journey to the Atlantic, they had covered forty-one states and visited 1,042 cities, given 1,836 exhibitions, and taken 100,228 passengers aloft in their planes. No doubt it was the first ride in an airplane for many. The flying circus also announced that they were operating in the East. While impressive, such outfits with their updated versions of Jennies like the Standard J-1 were becoming a thing of the past. There were also rumors of regulations limiting where they could fly and the stunts they could perform.

I had my angle and started constructing an article in my mind—out with the old, in with the new, if you will. Of course, eyes focused on their star pilot, "Big Jack" Ashcraft, Cowboy Aviator. I schemed. I had unofficially met Jack; soon he would meet me.

October 1925, Mitchel Field, Long Island, New York

Pulling my long leather flight coat closer and tightening my belt against the cool autumn day, I strolled amongst the airplanes and pilots at the airfield. Engines roared; mechanics worked on engines and yelled at roustabouts helping them. Officials gave instructions to those clearing debris, getting the field in order after the stormy night.

From what I saw, the event promised to live up to its hype. I recognized most of the civilian aviators mentioned in the article. I didn't recognize any of the military aviators except for the infamous Billy Mitchell and Jimmy Doolittle. Lingering near the racers, I felt my pulse quicken. How I longed to climb in one and take off. Only in my imagination could I fly 138 miles per hour. For now, anyway.

Male pilots weren't the only ones I recognized. My friends Frances Harrell and Ruth Nichols stood chatting by a Curtiss plane. Frances had moved here from Texas to learn to fly. She trained with the Curtiss organization. Wanting to learn all she could about flying, including how the engines worked, Frances worked in the shops but had recently started flying.

Ruth was an accomplished pilot. Educated too. She'd graduated from Wellesley College, where she also secretly took flight instruction. Ruth was from a prominent family on Long Island but tried to keep the fact unknown. She wanted her skills to speak for her, but as they improved and fame followed, more became known about her.

The three of us got together periodically for lunch. Tired of the endless advances and wolf whistles, which we avoided as much as possible, we earned a reputation for being "snooty," so I called the group the "Snooty Skylarks." After all, the men had their secretive Quiet Birdmen and their raucous meetings. Other women joined us when they flew through one of the fields on Long Island.

I waved to them and continued on my quest.

Thirteen-year-old Elinor Smith examined an airplane, deep in thought. I noticed a Negro woman I assumed was Bessie Coleman.

I walked over to introduce myself. "My name is Mavis

Perkins. I own a newspaper here on the island. Are you Bessie Coleman?"

The woman looked around. "Do you see anyone here that I could be confused with? Yes, I'm Bessie," she said, smiling, and extended her hand.

"Nice to meet you. Will you be in town long? I would like to write an article about you."

"I'm afraid not. I'll be leaving this afternoon."

"Shoot."

"Maybe next time."

"Maybe so."

I waved to a lot of people, and they waved back, but I was on a mission—to find "Big Jack," Cowboy Aviator.

I stopped to ask a roustabout where the Gates planes were located. He pointed right, so that's where I headed, taking time to speak to the few pilots that I knew. Then I saw the twelve bright red planes lined up. I have to say, the Gates Flying Circus fleet looked impressive even if their design was showing age. The twelve Standard J-1s were painted bright red, emblazoned with the star logo of their sponsor, Texaco, on the fuselage and on the bottom and top sides of the wings.

I spotted Jack, who watched my progress across the field, then pretended that he wasn't watching when I looked his way. When he saw me looking his way, he ducked under the engine and pretended to work on his plane, but I saw him peeking out to see where I was. In a way, it was charming. I sensed no pretense or lascivious intent as I had in some of the other pilots with their wolf whistles as I walked across the field.

When he was distracted with his engine, I quietly strolled over to his plane and spoke. "Hello. I'm looking for Big Jack Ashcraft."

Startled at the sound of my voice, he raised up abruptly, bumping his head on the engine cover. Rubbing his head, he responded, "You found him. How do you know my name?"

I pointed to his name painted on the fuselage.

"Oh, yeah. I forget about that sometimes. You'd think I would remember by now. Who do I have the pleasure of talking to?"

I extended my hand. "I'm Mavis Perkins, owner and editor of the local newspaper, *News Today*."

Jack wiped his hand on his coveralls and hesitated before he tentatively shook mine, grasping only my fingers. "Nice to meet you, ma'am. I've talked to lots of reporters but have to say I've never actually met the owner of a newspaper before. You're sure not like those hacks."

In Philly, he'd had his helmet on, which kind of scrunched up his face. That day, wearing a newsboy hat, he look different. I was taken by his sparkling blue eyes, sandy hair, and country boy demeanor. His smile, which was more of a grin, was very disarming. He wore white coveralls streaked with grease from working on his plane. And he was tall. At five feet eight, I'm tall for a woman, but he towered over me. It was no wonder he had earned the moniker "Big Jack."

"Nice to meet you, Cowboy Jack. They call you the Cowboy Aviator, correct? I'm interested in writing an article about you and the circus."

"Me?" There was that grin again. "My mother thinks I'm special, but I'm really just an ordinary guy."

I laughed. "I'll be the judge of that. I'm a pilot as well." Then I got an idea. "Have you ever seen the city and Lady Liberty from the air?"

"I can't say that I have. Not up close, anyway."

"I'll tell you what. You're at Curtiss Field, right?"

He nodded.

"Okay, then. I'll fly over to Curtiss on Saturday to pick you up for a quick aerial tour. Afterwards, we can go to lunch and talk more."

"Sounds good to me. Maybe I can take you up later."

"Jack, let's just keep this pilot to pilot, shall we?"

He blushed and nodded. He looked intently at me, as if he recognized me, then shook his head slightly.

"More than likely, we'll have fog early, but I'll get over when I can," I said. "Bye for now." I walked off, but turned back to wave. He was watching and waved back, then shook his head and went back to his task.

This is going to be fun.

Frances and Ruth were still talking and waved me over when I walked by.

"So, who was that?" Frances asked. "He's pretty cute."

"That's Big Jack, Cowboy Aviator, the one mentioned in the papers. I met him in Philly, and he took me for a short hop. I didn't tell him who I was, though."

"I remember reading about him," Ruth said. "You going to write an article about him?"

"That's the plan. It will be the old versus the modern. It will be about the circus with him as the focus. I'm taking him flying Saturday morning."

"Sounds like fun," Frances said. "What time?"

"The usual time. When the fog lifts. I would love for him to be outnumbered, if you get my drift and want to tag along."

The ladies nodded. "We do."

"I'll call," I said as I walked off, stopping at the gate to jot down some notes.

As I was exiting the gate, a man walked up to me.

"Hey, gal. I noticed you taking notes. Are you by chance the lady who started the newspaper here on Long Island?"

"I am. My name is Mavis Perkins," I said, extending my hand. I handed him my card.

"My name is Churchill. Ed Churchill. I'm the front man for the Gates Flying Circus."

"You know, when I first started reading about them, I thought to myself that they must have a front man who is a newspaper guy and writes their articles for them, because they're good."

Ed puffed up a little. "Yep, that's me."

Then my mind flashed to Philadelphia, and I recognized him as the man who'd led me to the ticket booth. He was a stereotypical news guy with a New York accent. Beneath a loose overcoat that blew open with each gust of the wind, he wore a rumpled brown suit and vest, wrinkled white shirt, and brown tie. To complete the look, he wore round black glasses and a trilby fedora pulled down tight so it wouldn't blow off. I imagined him in the newsroom, sleeves rolled up and secured above his elbows, wearing a visor, pounding on a typewriter while chewing on a cigar. Seemed like a nice guy, though. I liked him immediately. Not many men got away with calling me "gal."

"I happened to be in New Orleans when they came through. I was fascinated with them. Do you fly?"

"As a matter of fact, I do. Recreationally. I have my pilot's license."

"More dames are getting into it these days. I don't myself, and don't want to, but I'm sure interested in the subject. There's another guy named Daws who talks to the airfield guys and puts out posters, things like that, but I write the articles and stringers. I can read people, too. Sometimes I tell the fliers what they're going to do to get people's attention. They don't much like it, but they sometimes admit I'm right."

Ed amused me immensely. He seemed so sincere and earnest.

"Well, I'm on my way to talk to Jack and cover the races," he said. "He and I have hit it off really well."

"I just talked to him myself. Nice guy."

"He's one hell of a pilot, too, I'll tell you that. Here's my card. If you have any questions about the circus, give me a call."

"I'll remember that. Thanks, Ed. It's been nice chatting with you, but I've got to go now, too."

He tipped his hat and walked off. He paused and looked back at me, shook his head, then rushed on to talk to Jack.

CHAPTER 5
FLIGHT WITH JACK

SATURDAY MORNING, I looked out the window to confirm what I already knew. Fog shrouded the buildings. However, having been a New Yorker all my life, I'd learned to read mists, sort of. I looked up and around at different angles. From what I observed, I predicted that it would clear by ten thirty. I left my apartment in the city and headed for Long Island and Roosevelt Field. I stopped by the office to see if our photographer, Joe, was in. I wanted Ruth to take him aloft at the same time Jack and I would be flying to get aerial shots for my article. Frances would fly wingman. I also wanted to pick up my souvenir ticket from Philadelphia.

As I guessed, Joe was there developing film.

"Hey, Joe. How about an airplane ride this morning?"

"Sure. You think it's going to clear up?"

"I'm counting on it. Get your coat and I'll fill you in," I told him, then made a phone call.

"Hi, Ruth. Are you free to go flying this morning?"

"Sure."

"Good. Meet me at Curtiss at eleven?"

"Great. See you then."

I then called Frances and requested that she join us as well.

At ten thirty, I put on my flight helmet. I tried to control the inevitable stray strand of hair that poked out, but gave up. I completed the pre-flight inspection of my Waco, then repeated the process as I always did. I knew Charles had probably checked it out as well. Satisfied it was good to fly, I climbed into the back cockpit with Joe in the front. I started the engine and headed toward the runway.

There were wisps of mist that would be no problem for the short hop from Roosevelt to Curtiss Field and would burn off by flight time. At Curtiss, I circled the field, landed, and taxied up to the hangar. Frances was examining her plane, as was Ruth—but no Jack. I checked my watch and thought I'd been stood up. Then I saw him inside the building, looking intently at an engine.

I motioned for a roustabout to come over. "Will you please tell Jack that Mavis is here?" I reached into my pocket for the Philadelphia ticket. "And will you please give this to him?"

Ruth and Frances now stood by their planes, watching and waiting.

"Sure thing," he said, and rushed off. I leaned against my plane, impatiently tapping my foot. Seconds later, Jack came running out, waving the ticket.

"I knew I recognized you from somewhere. I just couldn't remember where at the time."

"For a minute, I was afraid that I'd been stood up."

Jack look at me intently. "No way. I've been looking forward to this."

I motioned for Ruth and Frances to come over. "I want to introduce you to friends of mine. This is Frances Harrell.

She's from Texas and studying with Curtiss in the shops, but she's been taking lessons too. Before we know it, she'll be on the Curtiss exhibition team."

Frances shook Jack's hand. "I sure hope so. In the meantime, I'm learning everything I can about airplanes. It's nice to meet you, Big Jack, Cowboy Aviator. Mavis told me that you're from Texas. Whereabouts?"

"Truth is, I was born in Oklahoma Territory and grew up in Kansas. In the service, I was stationed in bases all over Texas. Our press guy, Ed, started the Big Jack thing, and others latched on to it."

Frances laughed and winked at me. "The press will do things like that."

"Frankly, I don't like horses much and never roped a calf in my life. My dad had a hardware store. Motorized vehicles like airplanes and racing cars and motorcycles are more to my liking."

"I certainly understand that."

"How about you?"

"Houston."

"And this is Ruth Nichols," I said. "Ruth's the brainy one. She went to Wellesley College and studied medicine for a time."

Ruth laughed. "That may sound impressive, but my flight instructor called me a nincompoop."

Jack's eyebrows shot up in surprise. "Well, what does he know?"

Ruth laughed. "Sometimes I couldn't tell if he was teasing or if he was serious."

Then Jack whistled softly and looked at the three of us in disbelief. "I certainly didn't think there would be three beautiful women flying today."

"This is Joe Wallace. He does photography for my

newspaper. I thought it would be fun to get some pictures of our flight. Ruth and Joe will follow us. Frances will be wingman."

I explained our perspective as women fliers. "We've found that we get support from most men, but others think we have no business in the cockpit of an airplane. We get flirted with a lot. We're a tight-knit group and mostly keep to ourselves. Some guys call us snooty because of it. We fly when we can and when we can afford it."

Ruth looked at Joe. "Come on. I'm about finished checking my plane and will be ready to take off soon."

"I'll get a few shots on the ground, and I'll be right there."

"I'm ready when you all are," Frances said.

I ran to my plane. The others looked on to see what I was up to. "I'll take you high, I'll take you low. Fast or slow. Any way you want to go."

Jack laughed loudly. "Let me think about it." He looked my plane up and down. "What have we here? A Waco," Jack said. "I've seen plenty but haven't had the opportunity to fly one yet." He looked things over carefully.

"Relax, Jack. I've thoroughly examined my plane—but go ahead, satisfy yourself. You nervous flying with a woman at the controls?"

He grinned sheepishly. "Nah. The plane doesn't know the difference, and you have a sense of survival just like we all do. I always look things over out of habit more than anything. Been flying long?"

"Soloed last week," I said, then quickly allayed his fears when I saw the concern cross his face. "Relax. I've been flying about two years. I just fly flat and straight, though."

I motioned for us to get in. "Let's go flying, everyone."

He grinned broadly. "Yes, let's go flying."

"Buckle up tight. I don't want to risk losing you," I said.

"You do the same."

"Always."

Frances and Ruth walked to their planes.

"You know, Mavis says she doesn't like men flirting," I heard Frances say, "but she's really a flirt."

"Oh, she likes it. Just on her terms," Ruth laughed.

Adjusting my goggles, I knew that I could never impress a flier like Jack with my skills. Still, I wanted to make a great takeoff. Concentrating intently, I taxied down the runway and made a pretty good takeoff. I headed toward the Upper Bay, then to Liberty Island. Throttling back, we circled the Statue of Liberty. To me, she was most impressive from the air. Jack evidently thought so as well, for he saluted her.

We then headed out over the bay. I tapped Jack on the shoulder and wiggled the stick. He gave me a thumbs-up and took control.

"Buckled in tight?" he asked.

I nodded.

Before I knew it, he throttled into a shallow dive, then went up and over in a loop. It was so smooth and happened so quickly, I could hardly believe it. Jack looked back and grinned. I returned his smile but jokingly shook my finger at him.

"You okay?"

I nodded that I was.

I looked to see if Frances and Ruth were still with us. They gave me a thumbs-up. I hoped Joe got some good photos.

Jack then proceeded to do a wingover. Again, it was so smooth and happened so quickly, it took my breath away. I took back the controls with the realization that anything I did would pale in comparison to his skills. Nevertheless, I intended to complete the tour that I had planned. We headed into the city and flew above the tops of the skyscrapers.

Then I got a crazy idea. I headed to Broadway and slowly descended down the Great White Way. Frances and Ruth followed, but at higher altitudes. Exhilarated, I flew as low as I dared, aware of the commotion I was causing below and around me. I caught glimpses of people hanging out of windows as we flashed by. Some were screaming, shaking their hands at me. Others cheered me on. Once we were down Broadway, I quickly headed for Curtiss Field. Despite my excitement, I made a perfect landing and taxied to the hangar, my heart pounding.

Jack stepped out on the wing and jumped down. "I can't believe you did that. Can't you get in trouble?"

I smiled impishly. "Probably, but it was worth it."

He returned my smile.

Frances and Ruth ran over. Frances was the first to speak.

"How did you get the nerve to fly down Broadway? I wouldn't have."

"I would," Ruth said, "but I would have checked with Jimmy Walker first. When he calls, you don't know who your wingmen were, okay?"

"You got it."

"We're going to hold you to that," Frances said, and they rushed off.

I looked at Joe. "Did you get some good shots, Joe?"

Ashen and speechless, the photographer simply nodded.

There were more Gates pilots milling about the airfield, so Jack introduced me to them. Joe dutifully followed and took several more photos. I met Ivan Gates, who was very cordial. His wife Hazel was there. I learned that she was a pilot and flew him from gig to gig. Rumor had it that Gates could be bad-tempered, but I'd caught him on a good day. Clyde Pangborn, also known as Pang, of "Upside-Down" Pangborn fame, acknowledged me pleasantly. His signature maneuver was flying inverted for great distances. Beside him was Judge. The dog came over and placed his paw on my leg. I looked at Jack and Pang, not sure whether I should be frightened.

"Uh, what do I do?"

"This is Judge. It's his way of saying hello," Pang said.

"Trust me, you want to be on Judge's good side. Shake his hand," Jack said.

"Okay." So I took Judge's paw, shook it, and said, "Nice to meet you, Judge," as calmly as I could.

The dog looked up at me and licked my face. I wanted to cringe, but a voice inside told me to smile, so I did, to everyone's amusement and laughter.

"Well, you've met with Judge's approval, so you've met with everyone's," Jack said, handing me a handkerchief.

Others I met were Ive McKinney and Fearless Freddie Lund. Jack explained that he and Ive had a good buddy named Bill Brooks who'd taken off to fly in Nicaragua for a while, but they expected him to rejoin the circus at some point. Then I heard a familiar voice behind me.

"Hey, gal. How are you doing? I knew I recognized you at the air races."

"Hello, Ed. It's good to see you."

"So, Jack, how do you get all the luck?"

There stood a guy I recognized from the newspapers and from Philadelphia. "I believe you're the current 'Diava-lo,' Duke Krantz."

"You would be right. Nice to meet you," he said, and we shook hands.

"I get the pleasure of taking Duke up when he does his stunting," Jack said. "We have a pretty good system, but sometimes he likes to go rogue and do his own thing. Scares the hell out of me."

Duke nodded. "Jack's one of the few strong enough and skillful enough for me to walk on the wings of his plane. Bill here is a little easier to handle. He does stunts as well."

"Hi, ma'am. I'm Bill Wunderlich," the other man said. "Jack and I joined the circus at the same time in Louisiana. Jack keeps telling me I'll get to fly sometime."

"Three of us had a business selling and repairing airplanes between Shreveport, Louisiana, and Texarkana, Texas," Jack said. "Did some freight too. We were up to fifteen planes at one point. Bill and I also did some car racing. I had a Hudson."

"That's impressive."

"Not really. They were surplus planes, and business was just so-so. We did pretty well as mechanics," Jack said. "When the circus came through town, I knew that joining them was what I had to do."

"Our partner, Buck Steele, wasn't ready to give it up yet," Bill said. "We'll get him next year."

"I look forward to meeting him," I said, then turned to Jack. "I'll get my car and be back over in half an hour."

CHAPTER 6
AN EVENING ON THE TOWN

JACK and I had agreed to meet for dinner and a walking tour of the city. I took Joe back to the office. There, I removed my flight gear and ran a comb through my hair. Topping off my outfit with a woolen coat and cloche, I headed back out. For some reason, I was concerned about my appearance meeting him. He was obviously a country boy, while I was New York society and a working woman. Worlds apart, really. It couldn't possibly be that I liked the twinkle in his eye and charming grin when he looked at me. I was waiting for Jack when he appeared at the airfield. The look on his face when he saw me, and the way I lit up inside, told me that I had been mistaken. I did like the twinkle in his eye and charming grin. He wore a nice tweed jacket and newsboy cap.

"Wow!" he said admiringly, and then with effort, he turned his attention to my car.

"A jazzy auto, too. The cars I raced weren't this nice. I'm not sure what this is. A Bearcat, maybe?"

I nodded. "Nineteen twenty-three. My father had a client who couldn't pay him, so the man gave him this car instead. I fell in love with it and begged Daddy to give it to me."

"Your father *gave* you a Bearcat? My dad gave me a bicycle when I was sixteen, and I thought I was hot stuff."

"Daddy is a softy when it comes to his only daughter. The car was his present for my birthday last year. I've thought about selling it to buy my own plane. Then I came to my senses. He gave me a car and lets me fly his plane. I have the best of both worlds."

Jack proceeded to walk around my car, examining every detail. I was ignored for the next several minutes, intrigued by his interest in my automobile. He appeared unaware that I watched his every move. At one point, he left a fingerprint on the hood. Without hesitation or looking up, he removed his handkerchief from his back pocket and wiped it off, leaning down at eye level to make sure that the smudge was gone. I could tell that he really appreciated a fine automobile when he saw one.

"I take it that you like it and approve."

"You're dang right I do," he said.

"You want to drive it into town?"

"Do I want to drive it? You bet I do."

I motioned to the driver's seat. "Get in. I always like a chauffeur."

There was that grin again, broader than ever.

We got inside. He was like a kid with a new toy.

"How fast will it go?"

"About a hundred, I think."

"Have you tested it?"

"Once or twice, but don't tell Daddy."

"Daddy will never know." And with that, we roared off.

At my place, we left the car with the valet and Gerald,

the doorman, opened the door for me. His son, Wendell, sat on the sidewalk nearby.

"Thank you, Gerald," I said. "I want to introduce you to a new friend of mine. This is Jack Ashcraft. He's a pilot too. I showed him our fair city from the air this morning."

Gerald smiled. "Very fine, ma'am. Very fine."

"It's nice to meet you, Gerald," Jack said, and offered to shake hands.

Gerald looked at Jack, then at me. I nodded ever so slightly and smiled.

Gerald grasped Jack's hand. "It's nice to meet you too, sir. Mighty nice. This is my son Wendell. He wants to be a pilot someday. Is that possible?"

"It's possible. I met a Negro pilot in France. His name was Eugene Bullard, and he flew with the Escadrille. Here in New York, there's Hubert Julian. I've got to be honest with you, though. It's harder for folks like you."

"Yes, sir," Gerald said. "I understand. We're used to that, and we're willing to work hard."

Jack winked at them. "Then I think you'll get it done. Good luck."

"Gerald, would you please have a taxi pick us up at seven thirty?"

"I sure will, ma'am."

Jack followed me into the lobby and into the elevator.

"My apartment is on the fifth floor."

Jack looked at his surroundings. "I've stayed in a few places like this, but sure as heck never lived in one. This is nice—real nice."

"I'm going to take a quick shower and change," I told him. "Please, make yourself at home." I walked down the hall to my bedroom but peeked out the door.

Jack removed his hat and sat down on the sofa. He fiddled with his cap and looked around, uneasy.

"Feel free to fix yourself a drink," I said from the bedroom. "The bar is near the kitchen. I'm sure you don't get the good stuff when you're out on the road."

"No, ma'am."

"Pick something out for me, and I'll join you before we leave."

I can't be sure, but I think Jack tasted all of the liquors in the cabinet, for I heard several bottles being quietly removed and replaced. When I came from my bedroom, he was roaming my apartment carrying a bourbon. He left the bottle on the counter. A painting caught his eye, and he examined it closely.

"You like it?"

Jack started at the sound of my voice. "I sure do. The colors of the trees are just right. I don't take much time to notice these things when we're touring."

"I painted that a couple of years ago after my first cross-country flight."

"You can paint pictures too?"

I laughed. "If you want to call it that."

He turned to look at me. His eyes widened and he choked on his drink when he saw me.

"You okay?" I picked up a napkin and handed it to him.

He nodded. "It just went down the wrong pipe, I guess. That's what my mama used to say, anyway." He handed me my drink.

"Mmm. Sherry, my favorite."

He appraised my attire—a champagne-colored dress, pearl necklace and earrings. My pumps matched my dress.

"You sure look nice. Am I dressed okay? This is my best

jacket. I don't have much of a wardrobe, being on the road so much."

"You look fine," I said. "The place I have in mind isn't fancy, but it's a quiet place where we can talk. Shall we go?"

"I'm ready as I'll every be."

We were walking out the door when the phone rang. "Damn. Excuse me, I have a feeling I need to answer this."

I picked up the phone. I knew who was on the line. "Hello, Daddy." I rolled my eyes. "Jimmy Walker just called you, huh? You're referring to Jimmy Walker the newly elected Mayor, I assume."

Jack raised his eyebrows.

"The plane looked like ours because it was. I went flying today." Pause. "A new friend was with me. He's a pilot with a flying circus in town for the air races." I winked at Jack.

"Yes, I flew low. I wouldn't say it was that low, but maybe so. We were having so much fun." Pause. "Would you like me to call Mr. Walker and smooth things over?" Pause. "Okay, then. I'll let you talk to him. Tell him that I won't do it again without permission." I crossed my fingers behind my back so Jack could see. I heard him chuckle softly. "Yes, I promise I won't do it again. See you and Mother for lunch Sunday? No, I didn't notice other planes flying at the same time. They were probably just tagging along." I crossed my fingers again. "Bye, Daddy."

I looked at Jack. "I bet Joe got some great photos from the air. Guess I won't be using them in the article. Not soon, anyway. Darn."

The restaurant where I thought we might have dinner was nice, but not fancy. As a backup, there was a diner across the street called Saul's. When the taxi stopped in front of the restaurant, Jack looked concerned. I paid the driver.

I nodded toward the place across the street. "Saul's is delightful. I haven't been there since I was a teenager. I've been meaning to go back for old times' sake. Does that work for you?"

He nodded, relieved. "It works for me. I don't get paid until Monday."

"Saul's it is." I took his arm, and we crossed the street. Inside, we scooted into a booth in the back. I looked around.

"I don't think this place has changed a bit in ten years. Since high school. I think it has a certain charm." I smiled at Jack.

"These are the types of places that I know best. We don't eat fancy. What do you suggest?"

"A pastrami on rye or a Reuben sandwich, of course. After all, you are in New York. Anything but a hamburger."

Jack laughed. "The concept of sauerkraut on a sandwich never appealed to me much, so I guess I'll go with the pastrami on rye. I can't remember eating one—at least, I didn't know it if I did."

"I'll have a Reuben, then." We placed our orders.

"So, Cowboy Jack, you told Frances that you're not from Texas. Where are you from again?"

"Oklahoma originally, before it was a state. My dad made the Oklahoma land run on an old horse he called Bird. Then we moved to a place called Protection in Kansas."

"How interesting. And what did it need protection from?"

"I don't rightly know. Indians, I reckon. Wait—seems like Dad said something about a protective tariff or something. Kansas is for an Indian tribe."

"Do you have brothers and sisters?"

Jack laughed. "A passel. Five brothers and five sisters."

"My goodness. Your poor mother must be exhausted."

He nodded and laughed. "Your turn. What does 'Daddy' who gives his daughter a fancy car for her birthday, lets her fly his airplane, and knows the mayor of the largest city in the country do for a living?"

I laughed. "Daddy is an investment attorney and is known in New York and across the country. Around the world, actually. He's also an investor. Mother's family has interests in department stores."

"For the life of me, I can't figure out what you see in me."

I grasped his hands and noticed that they were a bit rough, but they were clean. He had scrubbed his nails. "I find you genuine. The real deal, as you would say. And you think it's okay that I fly airplanes. You trusted me to fly you as a passenger."

He looked at me earnestly. "Nobody in a plane wants to live more than the pilot. What got you interested in flying?"

"It's Daddy's fault. He made me try things to build up courage, like leaping off cliffs into water and jumping horses."

"That explains a lot."

"You want to hear something funny? I was dismissed from a private school for violating rules and another for 'behavior issues.'"

Jack roared with laughter. "I thought I was ornery growing up."

"I thought flying looked like fun. I saw it as a challenge. My instructor found teaching me a challenge. I wasn't a natural, but I hung in there."

Jack nodded in appreciation.

"Mother and Dad, especially Mother, set me up with men who are uninteresting and stuffy. They are usually stockbrokers. They think the cockpit is no place for a woman. Everyone wants me to conform to society's norms."

"Well, they need to spend time at any airfield."

"I have an older brother who is part of Daddy's firm. My younger brother traveled around Africa for a while but has settled down and is in law school now. The family has enough lawyers, so I decided to study journalism at Columbia and Daddy helped me start a newspaper. I'm grateful for that." I touched him on the arm. "Your turn. How long have you flown with Gates?"

"About a year now. They flew through Shreveport, where me and some buddies had set up shop. The circus headquartered in New Orleans for the winter. When I heard about them, I headed straight down and applied. I couldn't see getting old in Shreveport. Neither could Bill Wunderlich. Our partner, Buck Steele, will come around."

Jack finished his sandwich. I pushed my plate toward him. Hungrily, he reached for the half of my sandwich I hadn't eaten and ate it ravenously in spite of the sauerkraut.

Jack got a distant look on his face. There was anguish in his eyes, as if he had seen something awful in the past. "It was tough going at first. It was if someone had put a voodoo spell on us."

"What happened?"

"I probably shouldn't tell you this. You may not want to fly with me, but here goes." He took a deep breath. "I lost a passenger in Baton Rouge. A couple of kids wanted to take a flight with some simple stunting, something we didn't normally do, so I ran it by Pang. He said okay."

"Go on."

"I didn't do anything I hadn't done before. The plane was new, and we checked it out really well before we went up. We were only up about five hundred feet when I went into a spin, and I couldn't get out."

I could tell the mere thought of the incident still affected him deeply. He winced, then got a vacant look in his eyes and was unable to speak for several moments. On impulse, I took his hands and waited patiently until he regained his composure.

"I spun in. We crashed. One boy was killed, and the other was really banged up. I only had a few cuts and my arm was broken, but I was alive. The worst part was the case of the nerves that got me afterwards." He spoke softly. "I spent a few days in a sanitorium. Bill's dad is a doctor, so I spent a week at their place too. He got me help that I needed."

"That's awful. How did you get over such a horrible experience?"

"I haven't. Not completely, anyway. I don't think I ever will. I don't think about it as much as I did, but sometimes at night . . ."

"How were you able to fly again?"

"I was still at Bill's parents' when Pang paid me a visit. He told me that I needed to expect things like this to happen no matter how careful we are, but especially if we did something foolish."

"You didn't seem to be doing anything foolish."

"I wasn't, but some do. Pang said that the public was to blame as well. They don't want to see us fly flat and straight. They want to see and experience danger, even fatal accidents. He basically told me to snap out of it or stay behind. They were leaving in a few days with or without me."

"That seems harsh. Unsympathetic."

"Maybe, but it can't be any other way in this business. So I got my act together, and here I am. I'm glad that I have Bill. He's been a real pal. I won't take him stunting on my plane, though."

"I met Ed Churchill at Mitchel Field—well, actually in Philadelphia. Tell me about him."

"Ed really made it happen for us. He met up with us in New Orleans and liked what we were doing. He and Gates talked. He told Gates that if we were going to make it in the Northeast, we needed the works. Or the 'woiks,' as Ed put it."

"What did he mean by that?"

"He said we needed a sponsor so we could paint their logo on our planes to advertise for them and get free gas. There were vehicles we should get, like a canteen truck so the pilots and workers could eat at the field and not have to go into town. They could sell food as well. He said to get a fuel truck, a tent to repair planes under, a truck to carry it, and other vehicles. And a car. Everything would advertise Texaco as our sponsor."

"That's good thinking."

"Gates is a good businessman. He pulled it all together."

"And of course, we needed Ed to write the articles for the newspapers. I have to say, the man's delivered. We have another guy who contacts other groups like the National Guard about airfields. He has posters made and distributed. Stuff like that. Ed's become a good friend too."

"Gates Flying Circus really is the whole package."

"Yes, ma'am, we are."

Jack paid the check, and then we strolled along the streets and talked. We stopped at a speakeasy for a few minutes. I introduced him to some friends, and we danced a little, but it was noisy, and I wanted a short night.

We walked back to my apartment, arm in arm. At the door, he kissed me gently on the cheek.

"I really had a good time today. Thank you. Frankly, the dames—" He paused and chuckled. "—I mean women who usually come around aren't as classy as you are."

Uncertain how to respond, I simply smiled. "I had a good time as well. When do I get my turn with you in the pilot's cockpit?"

"You still want to fly with me after I told you about Baton Rouge?" he asked.

"Jack, you want to continue living as much as I do. If anything, you're more careful than ever."

"We'll go flying in a couple of weeks, then. We're headed back out to Pennsylvania for some exhibitions. Then we'll be back in town for the holidays before heading down to Florida."

"Call me when you return. I'm depending on it, hear?"

"Loud and clear." He started to walk off, then turned around.

"Will you help me do some shopping for my family? I'm going to ask Pang and Gates for time off to visit them over the holidays."

"I'll be glad to."

"See you then. Oh, you'll need this." He reached into his shirt pocket and handed me the ticket from Philadelphia.

I picked up the newspaper at my door. A photo and caption caught my eye, and I smiled. There was also a picture of Jack. The picture was of the fleet of Gates airplanes lined up at the National Air Races. The caption read: *The old guard of flying machines of the Gates Flying*

Circus isn't finished yet. The name on the byline was Ed Churchill.

"Jack." He stopped and looked back. "You may want this."

He glanced at it and smiled. "Thanks. I'll add it to my collection."

CHAPTER 7
THE SNOOTY SKYLARKS

THE SNOOTY SKYLARKS met when we could get together. These were usually casual affairs in some back corner of a hangar. Since the weather was getting chilly, I invited them to my office on Long Island. I brought sandwiches from Saul's.

"So," Frances said as she pulled up a chair, "Jack is cute. Did he flirt with you?"

"Of course," I replied, handing her a sandwich. Ruth was right behind her.

"Give us all the details," Ruth said, unwrapping hers.

"He wasn't like the others, though. He was kind of cute about it in a country boy sort of way. And a bit clumsy. Then I told him to keep our conversation pilot to pilot."

"What did he say to that?" Ruth asked.

"Nothing. Actually, he seemed relieved."

Ruth laughed. "As handsome as he is, he probably gets flirted with a lot. The girls were sure working the guys at the air races."

"You surprised the heck out of me flying down

Broadway on Saturday," Ruth said. "I thought it best to stay at a little higher altitude. Joe could get better shots."

"I'm glad you did, but I can't use them yet. Walker called Daddy, then Daddy called me. I did just as you asked and claimed I didn't know who else was flying."

"Thanks. I don't want to be grounded." Ruth laughed. "Or worse."

"My altitude was above Ruth's," Frances said. "I really didn't want to take any chances. It was fun to watch from there."

"Jack and I went out later. He hadn't dressed for dinner and hadn't been paid, so we went to Saul's. Afterwards, we strolled the streets and talked. The night was quite charming, actually."

"Are you going to see him again?" Frances asked.

I nodded, chewing. "They're going to Pennsylvania, and then they'll be back in a couple of weeks. He promised to take me flying then. I asked him to do some stunting. On Saturday, I let him fly the Waco, and he looped and a did a wingover. I didn't get sick or dizzy or anything, but I was sure glad that I ate a light breakfast."

We sat quietly for a few minutes, eating our sandwiches and munching Saratoga chips. Then I asked, "What flying are you doing?"

"I'm getting as much flying time as I can to hone my skills, but it's hard," Ruth said. "There are so few flying jobs for women. For anyone. Occasionally, I get asked to fly to promote something. I'm glad for everything I can get."

"I'm so thankful to Curtiss for taking me on," Frances put in. "They are keeping me busy for now. The exhibitions will be fun when I can do more, and I do think the demonstrations get them sales. Hopefully there will be more jobs in the future."

"I hope so," I said. "But in the meantime, women will be risking their necks with stunts and trying to break records when they can get a guy to give them the use of a plane. They expect more from us. Sometimes, you have to be twice as good as a man. On the other hand, women get attention and bring in sponsors. I'm glad that I have my newspaper. You all are good pilots, while flying is only a hobby for me."

Frances and Ruth nodded agreement.

"How many licensed women pilots do you suppose there are?" Frances asked.

"Around a hundred, I guess," Ruth replied. "Why?"

"I was just wondering if more women pilots would be interested in joining our group and forming a more formal organization."

"That's a thought," I said.

Ruth sighed. "We're not snooty, we just get tired of the snide jokes and want to be taken seriously."

"It would be nice to have an organization that advocates for women pilots," Frances said.

While Jack was in Pennsylvania, I had plenty of news to cover. General Billy Mitchell was being court-martialed for insubordination. He insisted that the United States was vulnerable to air attack and needed a separate air force. The military brass thought differently. Trial coverage was in all the newspapers. Writing the article for *News Today*, I took time to read the papers to track Jack and the flying circus. Before he left for Pennsylvania, Jack called me excitedly.

"When we went flying that day, I got an idea that I ran by Pang and Gates."

"What is it?"

"Well, I know you know about Billy Mitchell. A bunch

of us were talking with Hap Arnold the other night, and I thought to myself, *How can we prove Mitchell right?*"

"What did you decide?"

"We're going to simulate an attack on New York City to prove that the city is vulnerable to attack from the air."

I sat straight up in my chair. "You're going to do what? Surely you're kidding."

"No, ma'am. We're going to do it," he said. "Ed likes the idea. He's going to write articles for us and thinks the *Graphic* will cover it. He didn't think the stunt was your cup of tea."

"He thought correctly, but I'll cover it. When is this going to happen?"

"November 19 and 20. And get this—we'll be flying the same maneuvers the airmen used in the war. It will be great."

"I should tell you you're crazy, but I want to see this happen. Just remember—"

Jack laughed. "I know what you're going to say. Run it by Jimmy Walker. Ed and Gates have that covered too."

"See you Saturday morning after the attack. Be careful up there."

Jack hung up so quickly that I didn't have time to say goodbye.

I called an emergency meeting of the Skylarks, even though we had just met.

"You'll never guess what stunt Gates is going to do on the nineteenth and twentieth."

That got their attention. They leaned forward, anxious to hear. "What?" Frances and Ruth asked in unison.

"The circus is going to simulate an attack on New York City. They will use the same maneuvers many of them learned in the war."

"That will be great fun to watch, but why on earth are they going to do that?" Ruth asked.

"They want to prove Billy Mitchell right."

"That should do it. I'm envious," Frances said, and Ruth nodded.

A few days before the nineteenth, I picked up a copy of the *Graphic* to see what Ed had to say about what to expect. He covered it well. The first day, they would fly over Battery Park, then up Broadway. As a special touch, he said that Friday was a special day just for the kiddies. The article encouraged them to be outside to watch the airplanes and be sure to write a letter to Santa Claus, because pilot Freddie Lund was going to fly them directly to Santa himself at the North Pole.

I laughed to myself. *Yes, Ed knows to read a crowd.*

CHAPTER 8
ATTACK ON GOTHAM

Thursday, November 19, New York City

I WOKE UP EARLY, excited about the "attack." The *Graphic* had done its job publicizing what was going to happen that day. Only on ticker tape parade days had I sensed more excitement and anticipation. The paper said that they would start at Battery Park, where Texaco had corporate offices. Restless, I put on my coat and hat, and with a copy of the paper in hand, I rushed through the streets looking for what I thought would be the best place to watch the spectacle. I found myself near the Woolworth Building with thousands of other spectators. I looked at my watch—12:10. Five minutes to spare. They wanted to take advantage of the noontime hour, when people would be out. I had called Ruth and Frances to tell them where I would be.

Promptly at 12:15, four red planes roared over the tip of Manhattan. The street vibrated from the rumble of their engines. The newspaper reported Jack would be flying with Krantz as wing walker; Bill Wunderlich would stunt from the plane flown by Freddie Lund. Eddie Bond and Wilmer "Bill" Stultz would also be flying planes. Ed would be in one of them. The aircraft soared up Broadway, looping and doing Immelmann turns and falling leaves among the tall buildings. I shaded my eyes and squinted to see Jack's plane. I knew that Duke Krantz would be wearing his signature headband. My heartbeat quickened once I spotted him. *Stay safe, Jack.*

After about ten minutes of stunting, the wing walkers got out of their cockpits to perform. I could only watch Jack and Krantz. Out of the airplane, Krantz walked the length of the wing a couple of times. People around me oohed and aahed. He lowered himself to the lower wing and walked to each end and back. On the way, he "slipped" and fell, caught by a cable attached to his foot. Spectators covered their eyes rather than see a disaster, then laughed when they discovered they had been duped. Krantz then did chin-ups from the spreader bar and hung from it by his feet, then by one foot.

Through it all, I cringed, even though I knew that this was what they did for a living and they were in control. For ten minutes, the stuntmen thrilled spectators. Then promptly at 12:40, the men scrambled to the passenger cockpits and the planes headed back to Curtiss Field. I thought I heard a sputtering engine but wasn't sure.

"That was amazing," Ruth said.

Mesmerized by the spectacle, Frances could only nod in agreement.

I spent the day in the city to listen to what people said about the "attack." For the most part they marveled at the spectacle of the aerial performance. I decided to go to Saul's for lunch, knowing I would hear plenty there. As I passed by people eating sandwiches, I heard snippets of conversation.

"How in the world do they keep their senses doing all that spinning and looping?"

Another laughed and said, "I would be hanging my head over the side of the plane," then took a big bite of his Reuben.

This didn't do much for my appetite, so I tuned in to the guys in the booth behind me. "If you ask me, that guy in the paper had it right. Those planes could have been German or Japanese planes with bombs and machine guns."

"You're damn right. They could have taken off from a flat ship in the ocean or dropped from one of them dirigibles," his friend replied.

"If you ask me, Billy Mitchell is right. Damn right."

This same conversation was probably being repeated all over town and was just what the Gates organization wanted. I couldn't wait to tell Jack.

I stopped by my apartment to write Jack a note. *Jack, As they say in England, a jolly good show. I can't wait until Saturday for our flight. See you then — Mavis.*

I took the card to Gerald. "Will you please see that Jack gets this?"

"Oh, yes, ma'am. That was a fine exhibition today, wasn't it?"

"Indeed it was, Gerald, and thank you."

Friday would be a repeat of Thursday regarding maneuvers and stunting, but the focus would be on Central Park and Times Square. The day was children's day, and kiddos were invited to write letters to Santa. The paper reminded them and their parents that pilot Freddie Lund would personally deliver their letters to Santa Claus.

.   .   .

At my apartment, I jotted down a few notes about how the "attack" on New York exhibited how easily the planes could have dropped bombs and explaining where the planes could have launched. It was fun and certainly exciting to watch, but I agreed with the guys at Saul's. The flying circus had proved Mitchell's point, at least for some. I looked forward to the exhibition on Friday and flying with such a skillful pilot Saturday morning. And seeing Jack again.

* * *

On Saturday, I awoke to fog but saw the sun peeking through the mist. I determined that it would lift soon and that we would be able to fly. I bundled up in my fur-lined flying suit and helmet. Joe followed me in his own car.

Jack was waiting, anxiously looking for me. His face brightened when he saw me and my car.

"Mavis!" he exclaimed, rushing over. He hugged me and swung me around.

"My, aren't you feeling cheeky today."

He grinned. "Who wouldn't be? I'm going flying with a beautiful woman on a beautiful day!"

"I can't wait. Will you help me do a loop?"

"Maybe," he said. "Let's go!"

"Here's my ticket!"

We walked to the plane. "Your attack on New York was stunning, but keep it a little tamer with me, okay? I heard some guys talking at Saul's. They concluded just as you wanted. Mitchell is right. New York is susceptible to attack."

"Glad to hear it. I'll go easy, but buckle up tight. Let me know if something is too much for you."

"By the way, Joe wants to get a few more pictures. Is that okay?"

"Sure. Hey, Stultz!" he yelled, "you want to go flying today?"

"You bet I do." Stultz came running out but looked disappointed when he saw Joe standing by a plane waiting for him.

"You get all the fun," Stultz pouted.

I climbed into the front cockpit. Before Jack got in, he reached down and got a pinch of dirt between his middle finger and thumb, then flicked it before getting behind the controls.

"What are you doing?"

"What?"

"That dirt thing."

"Oh. Well, you probably know fliers are pretty superstitious and do all sorts of things for good luck. That's mine. I started doing it in France. I pick up a little dust and throw it in the wind. It's like us. We fly for a while, then come back to earth."

"Let's fly, then."

We taxied down the runway. Mostly we stayed over the harbor and the islands. After about twenty minutes, he tapped on my shoulder and indicated that he was going to do a loop.

I nodded and lightly put my hand on the stick to get the feel of how to perform the maneuver. Up and over we went. I watched carefully and felt the movement of the stick. The maneuver was exhilarating. I looked back and smiled, motioning that I wanted him to do another. After the second loop, he tapped me on the shoulder to tell me it was my turn. I nodded.

Taking a deep breath, I went into a dive, then pulled the

stick back. I didn't pull out as smoothly as I would have liked, but I didn't go into a spin and crash. I motioned that I wanted to try again. The second time was better.

Jack took over again and did some rollovers, Immelmann turns, and falling leaves like I had seen him do on Thursday and Friday. His flying skills and how smoothly he executed them at the controls took my breath away. After an hour of flying, we landed.

I jumped out of the plane. The instant Jack alighted from the plane, before the engine had even quieted, I asked, "When can we go again?" I was jumping with excitement.

"Anytime I'm in town," he said. "Let's talk about it over lunch and buy some Christmas presents. Hicksville is a good town for a guy like me. Gates is letting me go home during the holidays."

He turned to Stultz. "Thanks for helping us out today." Stultz waved back.

"See you at the office on Monday, Joe," I said.

Over lunch, I told Jack that I had a big night planned. Afterwards, I helped him choose gifts for his family. He was particularly sweet about picking out just the right shawl for his mother. We were having a good time and walking to the next store when something distracted him. Abruptly, he said that he had to check on something and that he would pick me up for dinner at eight.

THAT EVENING, I was deciding what earrings to wear when the doorbell rang at seven forty-five. Assuming Jack had arrived early, I opened the door. I didn't recognize the man standing in the hallway. The gentleman before me was stunningly handsome in a black tuxedo with a white waist-coat and bow tie under a wool jacket with satin lapels. A top hat and patent leather oxfords completed the look. All I could do was stare.

He held out his arms. "It's me, Jack," he said and spun around. "What do you think?"

"You look terrific, but I honestly didn't recognize you at first."

"Gerald didn't either. His boy Wendell was with him and didn't recognize me either. He sure is a cute little fella. I autographed a newspaper for him."

I was still in disbelief at Jack's transformation. "I don't know what to say."

"You've said what I wanted to hear. I decided to go all out for the night." Then he laughed heartily. "It took the guy a while to fit me. He wasn't used to all the bone and sinew, you know. I take it that you approve."

"Absolutely. Come in."

As he entered, I recovered from the shock of seeing Jack in formal attire. I was touched that he had gone to so much trouble, to say nothing of the expense. Inside, I spun him around once again, more slowly this time.

"My, my. What would they say in the Midwest? You clean up quite nice."

"Thanks, but seriously, do I look okay? This isn't something that I wear every day, and I don't want to embarrass you."

I took his hands, clenched them in mine, and smiled. They were softer, and his nails were manicured. "Oh, you won't embarrass me."

There was that grin again. "You look . . . beautiful." I wore a tight-fitting black dress overlaid with lace and with lace sleeves.

I changed the subject and tore my eyes away from his. "I want your opinion. Which earrings should I wear? I've always loved diamonds." Of course, I had decided to wear whatever he chose, and he liked the teardrop-shaped dangly ones. They would look great with my hairstyle.

"Pour us a brandy, will you? I'll be ready in a few minutes." I can't be sure, but I thought I heard Jack catch his breath when he saw that my dress was backless. When I returned, he handed me a glass. We laughed, crossed arms, and sipped the soothing liquid.

"What can I expect tonight?" he asked.

"Dinner. Then I have some surprises."

"Now you have me curious."

"Shall we go?"

At the outside door, he helped me with my long fur coat

that I wore for special occasions and cold nights. He put on his topcoat and hat. I have to say, we made a very handsome couple. Even Mother and Daddy would approve—of the appearance, anyway. A taxi took us to the restaurant. We chatted en route.

"Gates's attack on the city both days was spectacular."

"Thanks. I'll let Gates and Pang know."

"I was nervous knowing that you were up there flying. So many things could have gone wrong."

"It was a little dicey up there. The wind was gusty, and it was a bit nerve-wracking. It takes all I've got when Duke is out on the wings."

"I can only imagine."

"My engine started cutting out on the way back. A hose came off. It's a good thing I had a stuntman flying with me that day. I could have glided in or headed for the drink, but when I have people under me, I prefer to have a motor. He held it on until we got back to the field."

"I thought I heard an engine sputtering."

The taxi pulled up outside the restaurant and Jack paid the fare, removing bills from a monogrammed money clip.

The doorman took our coats, and we were escorted to our table. Jack left it to me to place the orders. He asked me about the steak dishes and how to pronounce them. He ordered the one he wanted, but I ordered the rest of the meal. Though he was a little nervous at first, Jack visibly relaxed after a couple of drinks. Acquaintances stopped by the table to say hello. Jack smiled congenially and told them that it was a pleasure to meet them.

Afterwards, we headed to the Palace Theatre. Rumor was that Will Rogers was in town and might make an appearance, so I had bought tickets. The place was full to capacity. Rogers was in the house, but didn't perform. At intermission, I pulled my press credentials to take Jack back-stage to meet his fellow Oklahoman. I knew he would be there. Jack and Will chatted, then he asked Rogers to sign his program for his mother.

"I can't believe it. I got to meet Will Rogers!" he said when we were back in our seats.

By the time we left the theater, it was after ten o'clock, still early by New York City standards.

From the theater, we went to a nightclub that wasn't officially open but would be soon. Texas Guinan, infamous actress turned nightclub owner, had returned to New York and was opening a place that she would call the 300 Club. We went through the procedure of going through a fake bookcase, knocking on a door, getting questioned by someone behind a small sliding door, and then admitted entrance. The instant we stepped inside, we heard clackers followed by Guinan's standard greeting.

"Hello, Suckers! And I never give a sucker an even break. Come in and leave your wallet at the door," Guinan said to laughter. "You may mean all the world to your mother, but you're just a cover charge to me." She shook her clackers louder.

Jack gaped at the woman. "So that's Texas Guinan."

I nodded.

"Well, I'll be. The whoopee girl herself. I've heard of her but wasn't sure if she really existed."

I laughed. "The saying goes that Jimmy Walker runs New York by day, and Texas Guinan runs it at night."

We made our way to an empty table. Jack's gaze was glued to the stage at first, then to all the activity in the room. Guinan strolled through the crowd and made her way to our table.

"And who do we have here?"

"This is Big Jack Ashcraft from Texas. He's a pilot," I said.

"I bet he can make any woman soar, if you know what I mean," she said with a wink and cackled. "In case anybody asks, this place doesn't exist, and you aren't here. Understand?" she said, and strolled back to the stage.

"Ladies and gentlemen, may I present Nellie. She's going to do a fan dance for your pleasure," Guinan announced. "She doesn't dance very well, but let's give the little girl a great big hand."

Everyone clapped while Nellie, holding two giant feather fans in front of her, swirled out on the stage, repositioning the fans with each move. Six other girls, three on each side, danced behind her. Nellie and the other girls danced for ten minutes. Then before she exited the stage, Nellie revealed her costume behind the fans—her naked body.

Some of Jack's expressions watching the performers were comical, especially when it was revealed that Nellie and all the dancers were essentially naked.

"I haven't seen anything like this since Paris," he said, laughing. He looked around the crowded room. "This place is something else. Hey, that guy looks like Eddie Cantor."

"That is Eddie," I said.

"Son of a gun."

Guinan shook her clackers. "And now someone who needs no introduction is going to sing a couple of tunes for us."

To Jack's delight, Cantor sang.

As the night progressed, we moved closer and closer to one another. I could feel the bone and sinew that he liked to joke about. I had never known a man so muscular. So strong. My mind wandered to the moment when he would take me home and we would say goodbye. I had insisted to myself that we would keep our relationship professional, pilot to pilot, but hadn't anticipated how attracted I would be to him. We were worlds apart socially, and Mother and Daddy would never approve. Perhaps that was part of the attraction—the appeal of the forbidden.

Laughing, we left Guinan's at about three o'clock and strolled along 151st Street to let the cool air clear our minds, then hailed a cab to take us back to my apartment. He escorted me to my door.

"I had a wonderful time this evening. Thank you," I said, hesitating briefly before I continued. "Would you like to come in for a nightcap?"

Inside, Jack took me into his arms in an embrace and a kiss that took my breath away. I helped him slip off his jacket, then moved his hands to the hook on the back of my dress.

"Are you sure?" he asked. "I'm just a country boy from Kansas."

"I'm sure," I replied, and we drifted toward the bedroom.

The next morning, I quietly got out of bed. Every Sunday, I met Mother and Daddy for breakfast. More often than not, they had invited some man that they thought would be an appropriate suitor for me. When I was ready to leave, I sat on the edge of the bed looking at Jack, waiting for him awaken. He stirred and looked around.

"So last night wasn't a dream," he said, and kissed me. "Look at you. Where are you headed? It's Sunday morning. Why don't you come back to bed?"

"As tempting as that is, I have lunch with Mother and Daddy on Sundays."

He gave me a pouting look that nearly disarmed me.

"It was nice for me too," I continued, "but you're not the first. I know I'm not."

"You're the best. Can you blame a guy for trying?" he said. "But I'm pretty certain Mother and Daddy wouldn't approve of our relationship."

"No, they wouldn't," I said honestly. "But I do have feelings for you, Jack. I need to sort them out. Then there is what you do for a living. A flying gypsy isn't compatible with any type of relationship."

"I know. You're different than the other women. They're dames. You're a lady, and I'm not sure how a guy like me would fit into your life."

"Let's take it easy and see what happens, okay?" I said. "We'll see each other when we can. How's that?"

He nodded.

"What's next for you?"

"Van and Hazel have a big Thanksgiving to-do planned for us, and then we're heading to Florida. In between, as you know, I fly home to see the folks. It's been a couple of years since I saw them," he said. "Come March, we'll head north again."

"Make yourself at home. Let Gerald know when you leave. Drop me a note now and then."

"I'll do that," Jack said.

I started out the door, then paused, desperate to be with him again. "I just had a thought. Have you ever been to the Macy's parade?"

"No, I haven't."

"Let's go, then. Meet me here at nine. You'll have plenty

of time to make it to the Gateses' gathering, and I can make it to Mother and Daddy's," I said. "Bye, now."

CHAPTER 10
THE FIRST AND SECOND GOODBYE

"HELLO, MOTHER. DADDY," I said, giving them each a kiss on the cheek when I reached their table at the restaurant.

"Well, I got things worked out with Jimmy, but then those fools with that flying circus wanted to fly everywhere downtown," Daddy said.

"Yes, I watched," I said. "I thought the exhibition was quite exciting."

"Wait a minute. Was one of those pilots that you took flying that day flying one of those planes?" he asked. "I guess that he's some country rube."

"It was and he is, but he's really quite sweet. I didn't encourage him, though," I said. "He's really a skilled flier. He told me they wanted to prove Billy Mitchell right."

Daddy smiled and nodded. "I have to admit, their flying was quite impressive and made a good case for Mitchell."

I nodded. "He took me flying yesterday."

That got Daddy's attention. He leaned forward slightly. "Did he do a loop with you aboard?"

"Not only did he perform a loop, but he let me take the controls and do one myself! The first one I pulled out too soon. The second one was okay."

Daddy became quite inquisitive. "What was that like?"

"It was like the earth falling away forever, then suddenly appearing again. It was magnificent, but difficult to describe."

"It would be amazing to be able to fly like that."

Mother alternately looked at whoever was speaking.

Daddy leaned more toward me. "What other maneuvers did he perform?"

"I tell you, Daddy, Jack did a wingover that was so smooth, I hardly knew it had happened. I didn't get dizzy or anything. Then he did what I think was a hammerhead. He did it instinctively. I would have needed more land markers. There were more maneuvers. A chandelle, maybe. I don't all know the names of all of them."

I slumped back in my chair, exhausted from reliving the experience. "The whole flight was marvelous."

Daddy slouched in his chair as well. "I would love to experience that. More so to have the skills to perform maneuvers like that. What we do is so tame. Do you think that he would take—"

"Ahem. I hate to break up this amazing hangar flying, but we are here to eat and catch up on what everybody is doing," Mother said. "While we're on the subject, though, I hope this thing between you and this barnstormer fellow is just about flying. I don't think he would fit in with the Perkins family."

I looked intently at my mother. "Jack is more than barnstormer. He's a skilled aviator. Anyway, who I date is my business. Trust my judgment, please? Now, can we just enjoy our meal?"

However, I knew Mother was right in thinking that Jack wouldn't fit in with the family. They would never approve, and Jack's transient gypsy life wouldn't work with my career either.

Thursday morning, Jack arrived promptly at nine. We walked to Sixth Avenue where the parade would pass by. I shivered and pulled my coat tighter around me, wishing that I had put on another layer underneath the coat. Though the parade was longer than the first year, it was still short, but people by the thousands came out to watch. Jack was like a kid again.

Jack pointed to an attraction. "Will you look at that? How did they ever put that together?"

Caterpillar Sam was the featured attraction at the parade. The creature had a human face with a one-hundred-foot body and wore a suit and hat.

Then there was Santa on top of the world. Jack told me that sometimes when he was flying really high, he felt like he was on top of the world. Bands played merrily.

I elbowed him when the New York Police Department's mounted unit passed by. "There's a horse for you, Cowboy Jack."

"I couldn't sit one," he said. "But they are impressive." He liked the animals from the zoo and told me about seeing some strange creatures when his parents took him to see the circus in Wichita. We were glad that the elephants didn't get frightened by the crowd and stampede. All too soon, the parade was over.

"Well, I guess this is goodbye until March," I said as we walked back to my apartment.

"I reckon so. My schedule is tight. From Protection, I

head to Virginia. I'm going to stop in Shreveport and talk to my buddy Buck about joining the group," he said.

"That's all going to happen fast. Where will you go from there?" I asked.

"Georgia, then Florida. Daws has us booked all over the place down there. He and Ed will keep us busy."

"Sounds exhausting."

"It is, but it has to be that way to keep flying."

"I suppose so."

He leaned down and kissed me tenderly. "I'll miss seeing you."

"I'll miss you too."

"I'll write and send you postcards now and then. How's that?"

"I would love that. Bye, now."

He gave me one more quick kiss before parting. We were reluctant to let go, and our hands slowly released until only our fingertips touched. He turned, and I watched his back disappear into the crowd. Rube or not, crazy lifestyle or not, I had fallen for the man.

My emotions were in flux, and I wondered if he had fallen in love with me.

Monday morning it was back to work. I was surprised when the phone rang on my personal line. Wary, I picked up the receiver. "Yes?"

"Hey, gal," the man on the line said.

"Hello, Ed. What can I do for you?" I asked.

"Hey, Jack's birthday is tomorrow, and we're going to have a birthday party. The guys thought you would like to come. I know Jack would like it. We've had a great year, so Pang and Gates want to celebrate that as well," he said.

"I would love to come. Sounds like fun. I'll bring a cake, if that's okay."

"That would be great."

"Can Ruth and Frances come with me?"

"Sure, the more the merrier. Wear your dancing shoes," he said. "The guys love to dance. I've got to warn you, though—they can get pretty rowdy. See you Tuesday at seven at Josie's."

One more goodbye.

The timing was perfect, though. My story about the Gates Flying Circus was hot off the presses. I devoted most of the edition to them, plus a few stories about the Skylarks. The article took longer than I'd hoped and included a few Skylark stories as well.

All of us assembled at Josie's. It was good to see the guys, and they greeted us warmly but got antsy waiting and wound up the old Victrola. The records were scratched, but the music coming from the old Victrola was passable for the crazy dancing that ensued. Sometimes, the girls and I danced with three guys at a time. Things were in full swing when Pang arrived, Jack in tow. At the last minute, I had grabbed my camera. I was glad that I did.

"Surprise!" everyone exclaimed. Jack genuinely seemed overwhelmed and appreciative.

I was surprised to see that Pangborn's jaw was bandaged.

He lowered the bandage briefly to speak. "We have some special guests this evening," Pang said, and the guys parted so we ladies could walk forward. "This is Mavis Perkins, Ruth Nichols, and Frances Harrell."

"Happy birthday, Cowboy Jack." I snapped a picture and gave him a quick kiss.

"Hey, where's mine?" the other guys howled.

"You remember Ruth and Frances, don't you?" I said.

"Sure do. Guys, these three ladies are damn good pilots, I'll tell you that," Jack said.

"They're good dancers too," another guy added.

"While I have your attention, I want to present to all of you the most recent edition of *News Today* devoted to aviation, primarily to the Gates Flying Circus," I said, holding up the newspaper for all to see.

"You'll also find a few articles about yours truly," I said, acknowledging Ruth, Frances, and other fly girls at the airfields on Long Island. "Thanks to Ed, Pang, and Van for talking with me about the history and to those of you who took time to talk to me."

Everyone cheered.

"And . . . I've brought each of you a souvenir copy," I said. "This one is mine, and I want all of you to sign it, starting with Ed—who, by the way, does a great job for you behind the scenes."

All the pilots eagerly reached for their copy. Ed nodded appreciatively when I gave him his.

"The gals brought a special cake with a red plane on it," Ed said.

"*Happy birthday to you . . .*" someone started, and everyone joined in. It was the best bad singing that I had ever heard. From the birthday song, they rolled into "*For he's a jolly good fellow, for he's a jolly good fellow . . .*"

Afterwards, Gates tapped his glass to get everyone's attention. "Jack's birthday is just an excuse to get together. We had a damned good year, and I thank you. That's worth celebrating."

"Hell, breathing is an excuse to celebrate," Wilmer Stultz said to roaring laughter.

Pang raised a glass of water. "Here's to the Gates Flying

Circus and another great year," he said, then replaced the bandage.

Everyone toasted with their beer bottles, and the rowdy partying resumed.

Stultz came over and held out four shot glasses to me, Jack, Frances, and Ruth. "Want a short snort of something more than soda pop?"

I looked at Jack, then at Frances and Ruth, and they looked at me and nodded. I looked at Stultz. "Sure, what do you have?"

Stultz pulled out a bottle of scotch from a pocket inside his jacket and poured a short snort into the shot glasses. Jack threw his back. The rest of us followed suit. I regretted it immediately. My throat burned and I choked. Tears poured from my eyes. Jack handed me a handkerchief. I dabbed at my eyes, then fanned my face. Someone gave me a beer to wash down the strong liquid. Frances and Ruth were in the same condition. All the guys laughed at us.

"How do you drink that stuff?" I said when I could speak.

"You gotta toughen up this gal to the finer points of being a pilot," Stultz said, and staggered off.

Dancing resumed. Rather than have partners, the movements were more of a frolicking group dance followed by a sort of line dance, but when the music slowed down, Jack pulled me to him and held me close.

Frances and Duke danced by us. "You two are going to have to go to a hotel or put on a faster song," he said.

Ed drifted through. "Hey, gal. What do you see in this galoot, anyway?"

The song ended. That's when Jack noticed a few guys missing.

"Some guys aren't here. I'm going to go check on them," Jack told Pang.

"I need some fresh air and have to leave. Why don't I take you to check on them and drop you off here on my way home?" Mavis said.

"We've got to go too," Frances said, and the guys moaned and begged us to stay.

Outside, I told Frances and Ruth that I would see them at Curtiss on Sunday evening, and we parted ways.

When they left, I turned to Jack. "What happed to Pang?"

"I'm not going to sugarcoat what happened. Gates slugged him. Shot at him, too."

I looked at Jack in disbelief. "What?"

"Gates is known to go on these benders. This was the worst. When we were at Bolling, he and Daws got particularly drunk. I heard a shot and went to check on things. Gates wouldn't let me in at first, but Hazel finally did. Pang was slumped over the sink, bleeding from the mouth, holding his jaw. I could see where the bullet hit the wall. Gates was in a daze. He said, 'My God, what have I done?' and dropped the gun. I grabbed it and hid it."

"Why would Gates do that?"

"Hazel told Pang later that he was kind of jealous of Pang because we all liked Pang so much and got along with him. He let it get the best of him. She reminded me that Ivan could have killed him if he wanted to."

Jack took a deep breath, remembering that night. "I had to smooth things over at the hospital so they wouldn't report the incident to the police. Ed took care of things at the newspapers. Negative press could have ruined us. Some of the guys send money home to family."

I suspected Jack was one of those who did.

Jack and I arrived at the workshop, where guys were repairing wings and other structures. Lights were on, doors and windows closed. Nothing seemed amiss. Inside, the guys acted drunk or were asleep. Jack sniffed and immediately knew what was wrong.

"You knuckleheads. You're high." He opened doors and windows. "Get some fresh air and sober up, then go join the party," he said.

We walked back out to the car. "They're good guys but can be idiots sometimes."

"What was it?"

"Dope? It's the stuff they paint on the wings to stiffen them. You inhale it, and it makes you higher than a kite. It's flammable too. Those guys were damn lucky."

"It works fast too. My head is spinning a bit," I giggled.

"The scotch might have something to do with that as well."

I inhaled a few breaths of fresh air, then drove Jack back to the diner. "Well, I guess this is goodbye. Again," I said.

"This time, it will be for a while," he said. "Before I forget, I want to give you something for that little fella of Gerald's. He wants to be a pilot like me, you know."

"Gerald told me how kind you were. You took the time to autograph a newspaper for him, then talked to him about being a pilot. That was really sweet."

"He's a good kid and he can do it, but it won't be easy for him," Jack said. He handed me a twenty-dollar bill. "Will you get him some books for me and give them to him? Maybe that will help."

"I'll be happy to," I said, touched by Jack's generosity.

Jack leaned over and kissed me. "Bye, Mavis," he said. "I'll write or send a postcard when I can. That's the best I can do."

"I understand, and I have my work. Goodbye, Jack. Stay safe, and for heaven's sake, don't get on Gates's bad side."

Back in my apartment, I warmly looked at what they had written. Ed wrote, *To Mavis Perkins, Flying Journalist. Thanks, gal. — Ed.*

CHAPTER 11
THE SNOOTY SKYLARKS BECOME OFFICIAL

THE SKYLARKS MET late Sunday afternoon at Curtiss. For fun, I designed and had printed a membership card just for us. I handed Ruth and Frances theirs to their amusement and pleasure. Frances had invited a guest who was quiet at first but looked on curiously.

I explained. "We are an informal flying club I refer to as the Snooty Skylarks. If the guys can have the Quiet Birdmen, I decided we can have our own group."

Frances read the card but could hardly control her laughter. "The bearer is a member of the vanguard of the surreptitious group of Snooty Skylarks. Founded December 1925."

Ruth took it from there. "And is a certified Snooty Skylark. She has mounted alone into the realms beyond the reach of keewees and willneverbes and should be accorded all gestures of friendship and aid by other Snooty Skylarks wherever they should meet."

Frances pressed the card to her heart. "This is great! I'll keep mine forever."

Ruth tucked hers into a pocket and patted it. "Mine will fly with me wherever I go."

"By the way, the 'attack' on New York was amazing," Ruth said. "How I would have loved to be up there."

"Me too, although I'm sure the wind around those tall buildings was tricky," Frances said, then laughed. "I didn't get any calls from the mayor the week we flew, so I thank you for that."

I smiled ruefully. "Daddy got a call from Mayor Walker himself, but he took care of it."

"Jack's party was a hoot," Ruth said. "My legs ached for hours."

Frances laughed. "Mine too, but I think the guys could have danced all night."

"Please forgive me. This is my friend Viola Gentry," Frances said. "She flies out of Roosevelt."

Viola and I shook hands. "Nice to meet you, Viola. Welcome to our little group. I've heard about you. It's nice to finally meet you."

"Same here. I can't stay long. I'm bushed and have to work tomorrow."

"Get this—Viola works two jobs to take flying instruction and to get flying hours," Ruth said. "I don't know how she does it."

Viola sighed. "It's not easy, but it's worth it. I love to fly, and I now have a license!"

"That's cause for celebration. How about a short snort, as the guys say? I know where they've stashed some."

I retrieved a bottle of bourbon from its hiding place and found four somewhat clean mugs. I poured a sip for everyone. We all gagged and laughed.

I looked at Viola. "This is something I ask every pilot. How did you get interested in flying?"

"I took a plane ride in Florida back when I was sixteen. My family was less than thrilled about it, and I got punished for it." Viola laughed at the memory. "They shouldn't have been surprised, considering I had already run away once and joined the circus."

"You joined a circus?"

"Sure did. When I flew for the first time, I remember feeling free from earthly bonds. Then I saw Ormer Locklear land a plane on the roof of the St. Francis Hotel in San Francisco. I was hooked after that. I wanted to part the clouds," she said, gesturing.

We all nodded that we understood.

"Here's another question I ask. Do you have a nickname? It seems everyone does," I said.

Viola smiled. "They call me the Flying Cashier. I work at a hotel downtown."

Ruth piped in. "I'm the Flying Debutante."

"I don't have one yet," Frances said.

"Then I'll call you 'Cowgirl Aviator.' Ed called me 'Mavis Perkins, Flying Journalist' the other day."

Every woman had her own story, but all of them told us it was difficult to keep flying.

"I'm always looking for a reason to fly *and* be paid for it. Sure, my family has money, but I want to earn my own way, my way. Nobody wants a woman pilot unless they need us for publicity purposes."

Frances nodded. "Yep. If a woman can fly it, anyone can," she said, her Texas drawl more pronounced.

We all nodded.

She continued. "I don't really mind, though, because I get to fly."

"I'm having a great time now. The Curtiss school is amazing. I can almost take an engine apart and put it back together blindfolded. I'm flying more. Some are telling me that I'll be asked to be on the exhibition team this spring. Then I'll get to go to different places and fly. Sometimes, I could stay up all day if they would let me, and if I wouldn't run out of gas. I'm keeping my fingers crossed."

"I know what you mean," I said. "I love flying on cool autumn afternoons and looking at the colors of the foliage."

"You certainly have to prove your mettle," Ruth said, "and not get insulted when you're called a nincompoop."

Everyone laughed.

"Sometimes I feel like I have to be twice as good as the guys," I said, "and I only fly recreationally." I looked at them thoughtfully. "I can't tell you how much I respect all of you. You work so hard for something we all love—flying."

I let that soak in before I continued. "I'm lucky. I get to fly for fun really about anytime I want because Daddy makes his plane available to me. I salute you, ladies."

"And you have a life outside of flying," Frances added.

Ruth smiled. "Well, I guess that makes you the snootiest of the Snooty Skylarks."

"I guess so."

Viola stood to leave. "Well, ladies, I need to go home and get some rest. Thanks for inviting me. I've enjoyed this. For the most part, the guys are great, but it's not like talking to other women fliers. I have my license, so now I have to think of a stunt to get people's attention."

"I'm glad you joined us, Viola, and I will have a Snooty Skylarks card for you next time. I'll also have wine to properly celebrate."

"I guess we're unofficially official now. We have a membership of four," Frances said, and we all laughed.

After Viola left, Ruth and Frances pounced.

"How was your big night on the town with Jack?" Frances asked.

"The night was wonderful. Jack was so sweet. He rented a tux, and I think he even got a manicure. He looked so handsome." I smiled, remembering. "He said that he didn't want to embarrass me, and he didn't. He was dashing. In fact, I didn't recognize him at first."

"Where did you go?" Ruth asked.

"Dinner and dancing at Rathskeller's. It's hard to find a place still open with Prohibition and all. He was quite fascinated by the murals. Afterwards, we went to a vaudeville show. He got to meet Will Rogers. Then I took him to Texas Guinan's new place that isn't officially open yet."

"Did you spend the night with him?" Frances probed.

Ruth looked at Frances. "That's pretty personal."

The look on my face gave me away.

"He was wonderful, in a sweet country boy sort of way."

"What's next?" Ruth asked.

"As you would know, he wouldn't fit in with the 'Perkins lifestyle,' as Mother put it," I said. "And he's an avowed bachelor traveling like a gypsy to flying gigs, so I don't see a future."

"But you're falling for him," Frances said.

Again, my expression betrayed my feelings.

Frances moved on. "His party was fun."

Ruth laughed. "They are a rowdy bunch. Somehow, I thought they were restraining a bit because we were there, but they were very sweet in their own way."

"What happened to Pang's jaw?" Frances asked.

"Gates got drunk and slugged him because he's jealous of Pang. Gates thinks the guys like Pang better than him. That's the short version to a very long story," I said.

"That's all I want to hear," Frances said.

"I agree with Ruth. They are very sweet in their own way. They would do anything for you. Ed calls me 'gal.'"

"It's a wonder he didn't get his head knocked off," Frances said.

I laughed. "With anyone else, maybe, but with Ed, I take it as a term of endearment. Maybe it's the way he says it, but I'm not offended at all."

"Where are they headed next?" Ruth asked.

"Florida. I can only imagine what they're like when they're touring," I said. "And I'm not so naïve as to think that there aren't other women."

BEFORE HE LEFT, I sent Jack some pictures that I took at his party. The holidays were a flurry of activity—Christmas parties, family gatherings, New Year's Eve parties. There seemed to be no end. Men asked me for dates, and I went on a few. They were pleasant enough but were boring, and my mind kept drifting to Jack. I would be relieved when the festivities stopped and I could get back to the newspaper. Routines and deadlines would take my mind off Jack.

Damp cold and fog enveloped the city, and I had plenty of news to report. There was always something happening in New York and in the aviation world. The city was always waiting for the next spectacle. I settled in to work. Late January, I received a letter from Jack postmarked Protection, Kansas. Inside was a picture of him and his brothers and sisters. I counted eleven total. There was a picture of his parents.

He wrote, *I had a great time with the folks, and my brothers and sisters. My little brother, Francis, to my right— we call him Franz—wants to be a pilot like me. He's barely twenty and learning to fly. I told him to get more flying time in, and we would talk the next time I'm in town. I buzzed the hardware store and the house to get people out, then did some stunting. While I was there, I took a bunch of kids and some grown-ups for short flights. I even coaxed Mother and Dad into the passenger cockpit. Dad clutched the side of the plane until his knuckles were white. Mother seemed in awe of the experience—or so scared that she couldn't move, I couldn't tell which. Ha ha.*

He sent a photo of the two of them in flight helmets and goggles, his mother clutching her new shawl about her. How special that must have been for them all.

It just takes a couple of days here until I get itchy to go somewhere. Next, I'm going to Shreveport to talk my pal Buck Steele into joining up with Gates. I'm also going to visit my Mason buddies. Then I head south to Florida via Virginia, North Carolina, and Georgia. — Jack.

To my relief, January passed quickly. To escape the cold, I thought about trying to catch up with Jack in Florida, but decided that wasn't wise. Instead, I traveled to Virginia, where Mother and Daddy had a cabin. It was still cold, but the long walks in the snowy woods cleared my mind. Having a drink or sipping tea afterwards in front of a roaring fire in the large fireplace restored my soul. The care-takers, Martin and Sadie, saw to it that I had everything I needed, but I seldom saw them, making the week very enjoyable. They were wonderful people, but I enjoyed my solitude at times. Then I had an idea. I wondered if I could arrange for Jack to meet me there in the spring.

When I returned to New York, there was a letter from Jack waiting for me.

Dear Mavis, Arrived in Florida okay. Buck joined us and we flew down together. On the way, we had a couple of nose-dives and took down some lines, the usual stuff. We didn't get hurt but were a little sore afterwards.

I had some tough luck early on, though. Pang had signed a contract for us to have four planes in the air. I'd been flying a lot, so I was going to sit one out. Well, they couldn't get one of the planes started, so they called "Big Jack" to do it. This happens a lot. Well, Eddie didn't have the switch right, and the darn think kicked back and broke my arm, but I didn't let on that I was hurt. Eddie's wife didn't want him to fly because she was afraid he would be killed. Guess she thought it was okay if I was killed. Four planes, we got paid. Three planes, we got nothing, so I climbed into the cockpit and took off. When I landed, the pain was so bad I passed out the instant I stepped out of the plane. I'm okay now.

My arm is in a cast, which gets a lot of attention from the girls—Jack had drawn a pair of eyes with one winking—but I'm finding no one comes close to you. Hope all is good with you. — Jack

From then on, I received postcards from him periodically as they crisscrossed Florida—Jacksonville, Daytona Beach, Tampa, Orlando, Ocala. In March I received a letter from him from Miami. Enclosed were a newspaper article and two photographs.

Dear Mavis,

You'll like this story. The other day, I was talking to this young reporter in Ocala. He was a bit starry-eyed, so I told him a tall tale. I told him that I was a captain and a test pilot in the army air corps during the war. You should have seen his eyes when I told him that I flew across enemy lines and was once injured in the foot.

Well, the kid took it all—hook, line, and sinker—and wrote an article. I thought you would think it's pretty funny, being in the newspaper business yourself. Pang and the guys gave me a hard time about it. They goaded me to tell them tell them more about my "heroic" service. Ed told me from then on to leave the newspaper articles to him. I told them, "The hell with you all, I'm going fishing," and that's just what I did. You see from the photo that I had a good day. I also told the young reporter that I could knock down a row of Coke bottles with a wing, but you saw me do that. Oh, I won a trophy in Miami for my flying.

I stared at the photos and smiled.

The Snooty Skylarks hadn't met since December when we had our holiday party, so we got together to catch up in March. Since my office was on Long Island, we met there. The big news was that Viola had found her stunt—she flew under the Brooklyn and Manhattan Bridges on March 14. When I heard about it, I bought a bottle of champagne to celebrate.

"Viola! Congratulations!" I said when she entered the office.

Ruth and Frances applauded.

"I bought something good this time. Not that rotgut stuff." I retrieved the bottle of bubbly, set out four glasses, and poured them half full. Then I distributed them to the ladies.

I raised mine in a toast. "Here's to Viola Gentry, and to her courage and determination."

"To Viola," the others said, and our glasses clinked.

Frances marveled at the thought. "That's amazing."

"What was it like?" I asked.

"I wasn't alone. I flew a Curtiss Oriole," Viola said, "so they required that Art Caperton fly with me. He's a veteran pilot for them."

"I've heard of him."

"We circled the Statue of Liberty and then started up the river. We zipped under the Brooklyn Bridge and were caught in vicious air currents. As we cleared the bridge, we were caught in a side wind from the west—rose high over the river for a minute—then ducked again for Manhattan Bridge, which was just ahead. We cleared that safely and flew off for Curtiss Field. I—a fledgling pilot with little solo time—had flown underneath both Brooklyn and Manhattan Bridges. As we landed, we were met by several of the reporters from New York newspapers, and I was so pleased when I heard one of them talking to Art Caperton, who said: 'It was quite a ride, but I'm glad it's over. Believe me, I was mighty glad to get out from under those bridges. The air was choppy. And that girl is a mighty good pilot, all right. I never worried about her.'"

"Weren't you frightened?" I asked.

"It really had not occurred to me to be frightened, but I sort of shivered later when I thought that if I had made a mistake, we would have gone under in our heavy flying clothes. We never could have been fished out of the river."

"Amazing. I'm glad no one had to fish you out," Ruth said.

"What's everyone else doing?"

"The same with me. I'm told I'll be on the exhibition team soon. I keep up with Elinor Smith," Frances said. "She soloed the other day. The youngest ever. I predict she'll get her license soon, and then we'll start seeing a lot of the Flying Flapper, as they call her."

"Did I ever tell you that Pang and Lund taught her to fly when she was about ten?" I said.

Ruth's eyebrows shot up. "That right? She learned from two of the best. I think you're right, Frances. We'll see her name in the news. I'll keep flying when I can."

I laughed. "Frankly, I just haven't had the will to fly much with it being so cold. I'm a fair-weather flier. However, I do try to get out a couple of times a week so I don't forget everything. I'll need to get tuned up big time come spring."

Then Ruth's expression turned serious. "My father isn't well, so I'm considering taking a regular job. There's one at the National City Bank that I've been encouraged to apply for. The position would be prestigious, but my heart is with flying."

"Oh, no!" I said. "When will you know?"

"I'll probably start at the bank next month."

Later that summer, I received a short letter from Ruth. To my surprise, it was postmarked Vienna. *Skylarks, I just couldn't do it. I need activity and adventure. I'm traveling abroad as a companion with a young girl to settle her nerves. We're traveling by plane as much as possible. In England, we hired a plane, tied our bags on the wings, and scooted from Devonshire to Scotland like a pair of modern gypsies. We had a small crash outside of Vienna, but I do believe the flying has proven helpful to her disordered nerves.*

This sounds more like Ruth, I thought with a smile. I couldn't wait to hear how that came about.

CHAPTER 13

ABSENCE DOES MAKE THE HEART GROW FONDER

AS THE FLYING CIRCUS TRAVELED, I received periodic updates from Jack as to their location in Florida. Late February, he sent a card saying they would be leaving the state in March. Their route northward would be similar to the year before: Macon, Atlanta, and Savannah, Georgia. by late March, they expected to be in the Carolinas. My heart beat faster when I read that they would be in Virginia. I plotted a rendezvous, but didn't know how to carry it out.

Then I received a letter postmarked Jacksonville in late March.

Dear Mavis, We'll finally be out of Florida tomorrow. Not soon enough for me. We did okay, but the weather down here isn't much to my liking. We had to do too many silly stunts to keep the crowds happy. Georgia should be good to us like last year. — Jack.

All day, I thought about how we could meet in Virginia at the cabin, or possibly somewhere else. With him on the road so much, I didn't see any way. I was leaving work for the evening one day when my phone rang.

"Mavis!" a familiar voice exclaimed.

"Jack! So good to hear you? Where are you?"

"We're in Columbia, South Carolina. Then Daws has us lined up for shows in North Carolina and on into Virginia," he said.

"Will you be in Fredericksburg, by chance?" I asked.

"I think that's one of our stops."

"Do they have an airfield? I've never flown there."

"Yeah. Why all the questions?"

I paused for several seconds and took a deep breath.

"Hello? Are you still there? This is costing me."

"I'm still here. I was just wondering. The family has property with a cabin outside of Fredericksburg. Would you be interested in meeting there for a weekend? Could you get the time off?"

"Hell, I'll just do it. I've worked constantly for months. I deserve a weekend off. Tell me when."

We arranged to meet in Fredericksburg the second weekend in April. I needed time in the cockpit, so it would be a good excuse for me to fly.

The cabin was free that weekend, so I made the necessary arrangements. The caretakers would pick us up at the airport in Fredericksburg and drive us to the cabin. There was a bonus for them if they kept the weekend secret. At the last minute, I asked Ruth to fly me down. We would share time in the pilot's seat. I didn't want to raise suspicions with Daddy as to why I wanted the use of the plane for the weekend. Ruth gladly obliged and found a Travel Air to rent. It was a beauty, red with off-white wings. I had never flown one, so it would be good experience for me.

With Ruth at the controls, we took off from Roosevelt at seven fifteen Friday morning. We flew southwest through light fog, but it burned off as the sun rose higher in the sky. By Wilmington, Delaware, we were in blue skies with wispy clouds. My kind of flying weather. I couldn't wait for my turn at the controls. In the meantime, I took in the fresh air of the countryside, glad to get out of the stale air of the city. I loved the warm sun on my arms and face.

Glancing at the map periodically to make sure Ruth was on track, I casually noted where we could land if we had to make an emergency landing. I looked for small airfields. All the while, I knew she was doing the same. I enjoyed the few hours before we landed in Wilmington to refuel and switched cockpits. For fun, I grabbed a pinch of soil and threw it into the wind before I taxied and took off.

In Fredericksburg, I made a pretty good landing with only a slight bounce. *Better.* We bumped across the grass field and taxied to the lone hangar. We arrived at three twenty. Jack had said that he should be there by three forty-five.

Ready to stretch my legs, I climbed out of the cockpit and hopped from the wing. "That's a nice airplane to fly. How did you arrange for such good flying weather?"

Ruth laughed. "Just darn good luck. I'll arrange for fuel and get ready to go back to Alexandria. It feels good to walk and stretch."

Anxiously, I surveyed the field. The caretakers' car was there. The driver waved in acknowledgment when I looked his way, and I waved back. I scanned the horizon for a bright red plane. I looked at my watch—3:34 p.m. My heart sank a little.

Ruth walked over. "Any sign of Jack?"

"Not yet. Don't you need to leave soon to get back to Fredericksburg?"

"My friends aren't expecting me until around seven, so I have time. I'm not leaving until I know Jack's here."

"I appreciate it, but the caretakers are here, so I'll be okay."

We both searched the horizon, and I paced. Ruth leaned casually against the plane, scanning the horizon and listening. Five minutes after four. I wondered whether Jack was coming or if I would be spending the weekend alone. Then we heard a plane approaching. The aircraft was a green Laird with yellow wings. The aircraft landed perfectly, then quickly taxied to the hangar. I looked at Ruth and shrugged. The physique of the pilot who disembarked looked familiar.

He waved and yelled. "Hey, Mavis, it's me, Jack!" He gave instructions to the airfield manager, then ran to me as Ruth looked on.

"Jack!" I rushed to greet him.

Big Jack swooped me into his arms and swung me around. Then we kissed. And kissed. Then for a time, we said nothing. We just gazed into one another's eyes, hardly believing that we were seeing each other again.

"Hi, Jack."

"Oh, hi, Ruth," Jack said, barely glancing her way.

Ruth laughed and yelled, "Bye! I'll see you Monday morning." When we didn't respond, she just laughed and waved us off. A few minutes later, she buzzed us, then headed north.

Jack and I ducked.

"Who was that?" he asked.

"Ruth. Remember? She's saying goodbye. I rented a Travel Air, and we flew down. I thought asking Daddy to borrow the plane might raise suspicions. I was beginning to think that I was being stood up."

Jack laughed. "No way. I borrowed my buddy Grantland's plane. I didn't want to ask Pang for one. I'm flying anonymously this weekend. I didn't want people in town to see a Gates plane."

"So, we're both clandestine in our meeting?" I laughed and I took his arm. "Come on, our car is waiting."

On the way to the cabin, the caretaker entertained himself by watching our displays of affection in the mirror and laughed. We didn't notice when we passed through town or the drive to our property. He let us off at the door, and we rushed to the bedroom.

At first, his lovemaking was urgent, even frantic, but then it settled into soothing bliss before we both fell asleep.

He emerged a couple of hours later wearing one of Daddy's bathrobes that I had laid out for him. I was in the living room, setting the table for dinner by the fire. I wore a pink satin dressing gown.

"Hello, sleepyhead," I teased when he kissed me on the back of the neck.

"What time is it? How long did I sleep? What's all this?"

"Seven. Three hours. Our caretaker's wife, Sadie, is an amazing cook. I'm finishing up a meal she left for us. Go pour yourself a drink."

Jack looked on hungrily. "Mmm, mmm. This looks delicious. Roast beef? What a treat."

Jack was as hungry as he was tired. There was nothing left when he finally pushed his chair back and said, "What's for dessert?"

"Peach pie."

"That's my favorite. How did you know?"

"Lucky guess," I replied, and set a slice of pie in front of him.

"You don't know how much I like peach pie." He handed the single serving back to me and took the pie pan.

Enveloped in a blanket, we snuggled on the sofa sipping wine after finishing dessert. Even though it was April, there was still a chill in the evenings. The warmth of the fire soothed us. The pops, cracks, and sparks of the flames entertained us as any fireworks display would have.

"Thanks for the postcards and letters. I loved every one of them. They gave me a greater appreciation of what you do for a living. I must say, it sounded quite grueling."

"I'll tell you this—I welcomed your invitation. My body's tired. Sometimes it just aches all over, especially when it's cold. I think I've broken all of my bones at least once. My mind's tired, too. People think it's all fun and games up there, and it is to some extent, but it's intense and straining as well."

"Tell me about it."

"Planes don't fly themselves. You have to be alert, looking around every second, and the planes are getting old. They are always breaking down, so you have to be listening too. It takes extra concentration when Duke is on the wings." He paused and shook his head.

"And the people. Oh my gosh. They can be so stupid. We have to watch out for them all the time. We have to pull them away from spinning propellers, or they would get chopped to bits. They try to climb all over the planes. Every once in a while, someone puts a foot through a wing and the guys have to do a quick repair. Kids like to get in the cockpits when we're not looking. People will even tear off pieces of the plane for souvenirs.

"Young boys swarm around us all the time when we're

on the ground. I'm glad they're interested—we'll always need pilots in the future—but sometimes I just want to tell them to go home. The crowds can really close in. I don't like their hands on me. Boy, did I need a break."

"I noticed a lot of this when I was in Philadelphia."

"En route from place to place, we have to be careful where we land."

"How so?"

"If we land in a field, we have to make sure there are no cows or keep them away from the planes."

"Cows?"

"Yep. The dope on the wings is sweet, and they'll eat the fabric right off the wings, leaving only the frame. Ah, such is the life of a flier these days."

We were quiet for a time.

"You know, that bear rug on the floor looks inviting," he said, and moved to it. He pulled the blanket over him and patted the space next to him, inviting me to join him. Our lovemaking was less urgent, gentler. Afterwards, he rolled on his stomach while I massaged his neck and shoulders. It took all my strength, but I could feel him relax.

"That feels so good." He fell asleep with me nestled beside him.

The next morning, I had a surprise for the Cowboy Aviator. I led him to the stables where our caretaker, Martin, had saddled two horses for us.

Jack looked at them in disbelief. "What's this?"

"Horses."

"Smartass. What's that on their backs?"

"An English saddle. I've done some fox hunting, and that's the type we use."

"It looks like a jockey's saddle, and I ain't no damn jockey. It's just a dang piece of leather. And I'm not letting any horse take off running. Uh-uh."

"Relax. You'll like it once you get used to it. Our riding won't involve running or roping a calf. I promise."

All the while, Martin laughed at our conversation and antics. He lowered the stirrups as long as he could for Jack, and he climbed on. The leathers could have been ten inches longer.

Martin laughed. "Well, you sure look like a jockey."

"Ha ha!"

The caretaker and I both laughed until tears rolled down our cheeks.

When I caught my breath, I told Jack the names of the horses. "I'm riding Jake's Luck. You're on Blaze. We'll just take a slow ride around the property. It's really quite lovely from the ground. It'll be a good change of pace for you."

Martin gave me a leg up, and we rode off. The horses were frisky at first because they hadn't been ridden much that spring, but they quickly settled down and followed a path in the woods and across a meadow with me in the lead. Jack's legs started cramping, so he took his feet out of the stirrups and let them dangle. I stopped periodically to take in a view. Lush green grass covered the pastures like a carpet. To me, it was like the background of a tapestry. Clusters of bright pink, yellow, orange, and red wildflowers scattered throughout the meadow completed the design. Birds fluttered in the treetops as if scolding us for interrupting their solitude. Others chattered to one another gaily. Small animals scrambled out of sight to hide in the brush. Deer watched us warily before running off, tails high.

Jack took a deep breath. "This is real pretty. And relaxing. I'm definitely not in Kansas, that's for sure."

I laughed. "It is lovely. I've been coming here since I was a child. I never get tired of the scenery, and I see something new every time I come. I hope the bears aren't out today."

Jack looked at me with alarm, then laughed. "I hope so too. So, this fox hunting thing. A bunch of you ride horses lickety-split through the woods and across fields chasing a little furry animal with a bushy tail?"

I thought for a few moments. "That's what it boils down to."

"Doesn't quite seem fair to the poor animal."

"I guess it doesn't, when you put it that way."

"You know what we'd call it back home in Kansas?"

"What?"

"We'd call it coyote hunting, and me and my buddy Troy would be on motorcycles."

I laughed at the thought. "Now that really wouldn't be fair."

On the way back to the barn, we passed an arena where jumps were set up.

He looked at me. "I suppose you can do this too."

"Of course! Jumping over fallen trees and other obstacles is the best part of fox hunting."

"Show me what you can do."

"Okay, but it's been awhile." I nudged Jake into the arena. We circled and performed figure eights so I could get the feel of flying lead changes again. Content that Jake would be okay, I headed for the first jump, clearing it nicely. The next five went smoothly, but a back hoof tapped the last jump. I patted Jake on the neck as we trotted toward where Jack stood watching. "Good boy."

"I'm impressed," Jack said.

"Don't be. The horse does all the work, but you do have to have confidence in each other."

"Let's get back to the house and eat. I'm starved."

We handed the reins to Martin, then walked to the house. Sadie had prepared a fabulous brunch for us. Again, Jack ate as if he hadn't eaten in a week.

"You're going to eat me out of house and home."

He grinned sheepishly. "I seldom get good food like this, and when I do, I don't know when I will again."

We spent the rest of the day paddling on the lake, then sitting on the porch talking. At dusk, we watched fireflies flicker in the trees. He told me stories of his travels. One was really cute. In his barnstorming days and even now when he flew alone, he would fly over a community to see what response he got from the citizens. If some came running out, he would land to take folks on a ride. He also conned kids into getting gas for him while he took up customers.

He remembered two kids in particular. "I promised them I'd give them a ride but ran out of time. I felt bad, but they were expecting me at our next stop. When I tried to leave without giving them a ride, the little girl would have none of it. She stomped her foot and threatened to send the law after me. Or her mother. I didn't want either one, so I gave them a flight and stayed up longer than usual. It was such a treat to watch them, I gave them a refund."

Jack told me about their engagement in Coatesville, Pennsylvania. They had just landed and tied the airplanes down when a dirigible, the USS *Shenandoah*, flew over. Quickly, they got back into their planes and took off. Jack flew next to and around the zeppelin, doing some simple stunting. The crew clapped for the performance, and he waved to them, then landed.

"The next day, we learned that it had crashed, killing fourteen crew members, including the captain."

"I remember reading about that. What an experience."

"We didn't know anyone personally, but we fliers are like a fraternity. It was tough news to take."

That evening after supper, before we went to bed, I put slow music on the Victrola and motioned for Jack to dance with me.

He smiled. "You're determined to make a dancer out of me yet, aren't you? You're trying to domesticate me."

I smiled. "Never. Just new experiences."

He took my hand, and I twirled, then leaned back into him. He pulled me close, and we swayed with the music. "It's hard for me to move my 'bone and sinew' gracefully."

"You're doing fine. You haven't stepped on my toes yet. Believe me, I would let you know."

The next morning, Jack was sleeping soundly, so before breakfast, I dressed and went for another ride. Riding the day before had reminded me how much I missed the sport. Sadie was just arriving at the house. "Put on some riding clothes and come ride with me."

"How about breakfast?"

"Breakfast can wait. Jack's still asleep."

At the arena, we each took a turn on the course. Blaze kept balking at a particular jump, so I offered Sadie a few suggestions. She circled once more, cleared the jump, and completed the course. We hadn't noticed Jack at the fence. We trotted over.

"Good morning, Cowboy Jack," I said. "This is Sadie, Martin's wife. I taught them both to ride so that they could exercise the horses."

Jack looked at Sadie and laughed. "It's a tough job you two have."

Sadie smiled. "Somebody's got to do it, and we do our best. The Perkins family is very good to us. And by the way, I know you're not here, but I'll go cook breakfast for you."

"No, ma'am. I've had such a swell time, and you've fixed some great meals for us. I'm fixin' breakfast for everyone. I'll make the best flapjacks you'll ever eat. That's what we called them in Kansas."

"What a treat," Sadie said. "I'll let Martin know."

Back at the house, Jack was in the kitchen. With a dish towel hanging from his right back pocket and one over his left shoulder, he furiously stirred the pancake batter. "You can't have any lumps, you know. Sit down, and I'll have some ready shortly."

Sadie and I set the table that Martin had placed on the patio. The three of us sat down and waited to be served. At the first bite, we agreed with Jack that his pancakes were the best we had ever eaten. We chatted merrily while we ate. Jack ate until he got tired of mixing batter or ran out of flour; we couldn't tell which.

"How did you learn to cook such a good breakfast?" I asked.

"With ten brothers and sisters in the house, sometimes Mother was just too tuckered out to cook and feed us all. It wore out my two older sisters, Lillian and Audrey, too. We bought wheat and ground our own flour, and a neighbor to the south sold us milk and eggs. So I made pancakes."

"We thank you for the breakfast and company, but you two go have some fun," Sadie said. "We'll clean up and come back later to make dinner. There are ingredients in the refrigerator for sandwiches for lunch."

. . .

That evening, since we had to be at the airport early the next morning, we were content to lie in one another's arms and talk, watching fireflies. The weekend had gone much too quickly, but it had been the time off from our routines that we both needed.

The next morning, we rode the airport, chatting about upcoming activities. Sadie joined us for the drive. Ruth was waiting for me. The Laird was on the field, ready to go.

"Thank you for everything, Martin," I said, handing him two hundred-dollar bills.

"Really, you don't have to do this," he said.

"This was the agreement."

Martin nodded. "Thank you. We can always use the extra money. We tuck away as much as we can." He took the money and handed it to Sadie, who put the bills in her pocketbook.

"Wise people. Bye, now. See you next time."

Jack and I walked toward the planes.

"It's nice to see you again, Ruth," Jack said when she walked over. "I apologize for being so rude the other day."

Ruth laughed and waved him off. "Don't worry about it. I'll go check out the plane again, but first, I want to ask your opinion about that." She pointed to the northeast, where the sky was darkening. "How fast do you think it's moving?"

Jack and I looked to where Ruth pointed. "Hard to tell, but it doesn't look good. I think you'll be okay until Baltimore, but be prepared to set down any time after that. There are a few small fields."

"That's what I was thinking. I noticed a few on our way down. I know Alexandria. That's where I stayed this weekend." She looked at me. "I'll have things ready in just a few minutes," she said, and walked away.

Jack took me into his arms and kissed me, then spoke softly. "Goodbye, Mavis. This was the best weekend of my life. Thank you."

"Me too. You look relaxed and rested. Do keep in touch."

He nodded and walked to his plane. Even though Ruth had checked out the plane, I did as well. Dumping my belongings in the front cockpit, I climbed into the cockpit behind Ruth. Soon we were winging our way to New York as we had planned.

What did this weekend mean for me and Jack? I had no idea. All I knew is that I had so much fun when I was with him. He truly lived life to its fullest.

Just as Jack and Ruth had predicted, the weather got nasty as we approached Alexandria. The rain pelted us harder the closer we got. I had never flown in weather so severe, but Ruth kept giving me a thumbs-up to reassure me. I tried to wipe my goggles with my scarf, which of course was useless. Eventually, the rain came down so heavily I couldn't see. We had no choice but to land.

South of Baltimore, Ruth spotted a small airfield and pointed down. She moved her hand from left to right, confirming the direction of the wind. Then she held both hands up and brought them together, telling me the runway was short. She held up one finger. I had one chance to land. My heart pounded. Nothing Charles had taught me had prepared me for situations like this.

Never had I been so frightened in my life. Concentrating on the task at hand helped. Throttling back, I descended quickly. I thought I saw someone waving a light at the end of the airfield, so I had an imaginary straight line and focused on it. I crabbed down the line, then smashed down the right rudder with as much resistance as I could muster, more than I ever had needed to before. Gripping the stick with both hands so I wouldn't slip, I followed right rudder with left aileron to get parallel to the airfield and set the aircraft down. Somehow, I kept the left wing from flying up, and we set down, bouncing down the airfield. At one point, the left wheel careened up but settled back down. I struggled to maintain control while I checked my surroundings.

Ruth was rattling around in the front seat, clinging to the sides. Someone in the distance was still motioning with the light, so I continued in that direction. The wind was blowing ferociously, buffeting us about. Rain came down in sheets. Lightning revealed a small hangar. The plane hit a puddle and stopped abruptly. The nose pitched down, but to my relief, the tail slowly dropped back down. Relieved that we were on the ground, I slumped in the cockpit, exhausted. Ruth shook me, bringing me to my senses.

"We've got to push the plane in as far as we can!"

The man with the light pulled while we pushed the plane into the hangar. We couldn't get the aircraft completely in, but most of the plane, except for the tail, was sheltered from the onslaught of the storm. The attendant threw a tarp over the cockpits, then motioned for us to follow him.

Inside, we pulled off our helmets and goggles and shook water from our coveralls. Immediately, we started shivering.

The man, who was really not much more than a boy, looked at us in disbelief. "My gosh, I wasn't expecting girls! Occasionally guys get caught in storms and land, but not women!"

"Well, I guess this is a first for you and me, actually," I

said. "I'm Mavis." We shook hands. Mine was still shaking. He noticed.

"It's a real toad strangler out there. It must have been quite a ride coming down out of that," he said. "I've seen guys flip planes in weather like this."

"It was—and I'm not going to lie, it was dicey—but Mavis pulled it off. I'm Ruth."

"I'm Milton, and I don't have much in the way of accommodations for ladies, but you're welcome to what I have."

"Thank you, Milton. We don't need anything special," I said. "Maybe a place to hang our flight suits to dry and a simple place to rest?"

"Sure thing. Let's see. You can hang your coveralls on the nails over there by the stove. They should be fairly dry by morning. I'll throw a few more logs in to get the fire going more. I'll put some coffee on the stove too. If you want something to settle your nerves, it's up in the cabinet. All I have to eat is peanuts."

"That would be grand," Ruth said. "We sure thank you for your kind hospitality. I don't know what we would have done if we hadn't spotted your airfield."

"You're welcome. Glad I could help. You're welcome to sleep on the sofa over there in the corner. It's none too clean, though. I'll try to find a couple of blankets."

"I'll check the plane to see if anything is stashed in it," Ruth said.

She returned carrying our bags. "By some miracle, these aren't soaked. My clothes seem dry—or at least drier."

We hung a change of clothes to dry, then huddled shivering around the stove holding mugs of coffee. The room was small, so the stove warmed the room in spite of the drafts. Milton returned with a blanket. "I'll be in the back office if you need me. Make yourself at home," he said, and retreated to the office.

"I have to tell you, that was one heck of a landing," Ruth said. "You kept your composure. That's the important thing."

My body still shook, but it was slowly subsiding. "Thanks. That means a lot coming from you. I've never flown in conditions like this before. I was so scared. I wasn't sure what to do. I just flew by the seat of my pants, as the saying goes. Thank goodness for hangar flying."

We then leaned back on the sofa and each other, blanket around us, and soon fell fast asleep.

The next morning, Milton fueled the plane for us, and Ruth and I did flight checks. Miraculously, the plane was undamaged except for a tear here and there. We looked a fright, but we were dry and the morning was warm. Thankfully, all we saw was blue skies.

Then Ruth turned to me. "We've both ridden horseback and have had bad experiences, haven't we?"

I nodded and got into the pilot's seat.

GATES FLYING CIRCUS, with Jack as its star performer, again toured the Northeast, including extensive tours in New York and Pennsylvania. Jack wrote me a short note after our weekend in Virginia. He thanked me and told me that he enjoyed our time together, but not much more about that. He mentioned that he was happy his pal Buck Steele was around and that they were making plans, but he didn't go into detail.

Another friend he'd made when he first joined the joined the circus, "Whispering Bill" Brooks, was rejoining Gates. Brooks had been flying for the Nicaraguan government in a revolt against their new president. The US had sent troops to preserve order after the uprising. Jack guessed Bill was no longer needed down there and was anxious to see his old pal. Jack said that other fliers had called him, Ive McKinney, and "Whispering Bill" the Three Musketeers.

From then on, I heard little from Jack but tracked their appearances in the paper. They were on the go constantly, either performing or flying to the next engagement.

However, I did receive an invitation to come see them in Syracuse.

Dear Mavis, If you've been watching the papers, you know how busy I've been. I'm exhausted but got to keep going. We're going to be in Syracuse and surrounding area for several days in August. Why don't you come up and watch the show? It would be good to see you. Be sure to bring your souvenir ticket from Philadelphia. — Jack

The invitation sounded like fun, and I needed a break. The paper was doing well. I had a partner, but I was managing editor and had worked nonstop since I'd returned from Virginia. The landing in Virginia had given me a great deal of confidence regarding my flying. This time, I prepared for my time off and was bold in asking Daddy for the Waco for the weekend to get in some real flight time. He agreed. I would leave Friday.

Most of my flights had been shorter, and I'd always had something of a cavalier attitude about flying. I had always assumed the weather would cooperate and that if I had engine trouble, I would have a perfect place to land, and someone would be there to fix my engine. No more. After Virginia, I paid more attention to everything a pilot is supposed to. I stopped over in Binghamton to check things out and refuel, then flew on into Syracuse.

The airfield was hopping. I took what I understood was my place in line to land. When it came my turn, I crossed my fingers that I wouldn't hop, or worse, ground loop when I landed. I spiraled down and, thankfully, my landing was pretty good. An airport official directed me to a place to park my plane according to signage: *Participants, right; spectators, left.* I taxied left and made sure my plane was secured before I left to look for Jack. I had just finished when I heard a loud "Hellooo, Mavis."

Jack raced over, picked me up, and swirled me around as he liked to do. Then he gave me a quick kiss.

"I thought I recognized that Waco coming in."

"You were right. This time, I just told Daddy that I was taking it. He didn't ask questions."

I took his arm, and we walked back to the hangar. "How have you been?"

"Great—but busy, busy, busy. Business is good. Real good. And you?"

"Busy as well. The paper is doing really well. I've brought on a partner, but my stake is larger and I'm managing editor. Readership is expanding. Advertising is up. Subscriptions have increased."

"Glad to hear it. Look, I've got to run. Get in line for your flight with me when it's time. They're expecting you," he said, and I showed him the infamous ticket. "Where are you staying?"

"Hotel Syracuse."

"Great. I'll come get you this evening after we shut down. We'll grab a bite to eat. It may be eight or so when I get there, and it'll be a short night."

"I understand. See you then."

After my ride, I went to the hotel to freshen up. I felt dirty and windblown, but the day had been exhilarating, first flying in and then all of the activity. For the first time, I felt like a part of the aviation community. The event was even bigger than Philadelphia the year before.

Jack came to the hotel when he said he would. He looked exhausted, and I told him so.

"I am tired. This afternoon, I alone took up four or five hundred passengers. It seemed all of Syracuse wanted to fly today. The boys couldn't get them in and out fast enough."

We went to dinner and chatted, but Jack had to get back to the airfield to prepare for the next day.

When I exited the hotel the next morning, the circus had just started its ballyhoo. The planes zipped around so quickly, I couldn't tell which one was Jack. Then a plane soared low directly over the hotel and waggled its wings. I waved as it headed back to the airport.

Once more, I watched the show and marveled at the skill and precision of the aviators. They had fine-tuned their routines even more. The spectators in the stands around me couldn't get enough. When Jack left, I knew he was going to land to get Duke, so I waited a few minutes to watch the amazing stuntman, then walked to the VIP/press room to get some relief from the sun and heat. Gates personnel greeted me as they drifted in and out.

"Hey, gal. I didn't know you were coming today."

"Ed! I'm doing great! And you?"

"Can't complain. Wouldn't change a damn thing if I did. You here for the weekend?"

"No, just the day. That's the plan for now, anyway." I winked at him.

"Well, I gotta go keep the guys in line. Good to see you."

"Good to see you too."

Outside, Al motioned Jack out of the lineup to the periphery of the field. I followed. Pang came running over. "Hello, Mavis. Nice to see you."

"You as well."

"What's up?" Jack asked.

"We're doing a land office business today. The whole

week's been good. Gates wants to celebrate to thank the guys and VIPs. He wants you and Buck to go to Hammondsport to pick up some champagne for a party tomorrow afternoon. He has contacts there and has made all of the arrangements."

Jack grinned. "Now that's an offer I can't refuse. I'll get fueled up."

At the fuel truck, Jack turned to me. "I just got an idea. Come with me. Get in and duck down out of sight until we're in the air. I think there's a blanket back there you can put over you."

Next thing I knew, I was in the cockpit, and Jack had pushed me down in the seat. He found a dirty blanket and pulled it over me. I choked and nearly smothered until we were airborne.

Once aloft, I sat up and took in the cool, fresh air. Buck looked over and shook his head. Jack shrugged as if to say, "What's the problem?"

The scenery was magnificent. The flight path was directly over the Finger Lakes, which were stunning from the air. The water mirrored our plane and the hills and trees and wispy clouds that floated in the cerulean sky. The light of the late afternoon sun glinted off the surface of the water. I had never seen the lakes from the air and vowed to return to fly over them myself.

All too soon, we arrived in Hammondsport. Gates's contact met us at the airport and had the cases of champagne ready. Quickly, they were loaded into the planes and the aircraft refueled. We readied to leave. Jack looked in Buck's plane and put a couple more cases in the front cockpit from his. Buck looked on suspiciously. "What the h—"

Jack interrupted. "You know what, Buck? I've never

been to Hammondsport, so Mavis and I are going to check it out. We'll come along a little later."

"Pang's not going to like that," Buck answered.

"I give you my word, I'll make it back in time for the party. I always do. It's not until tomorrow anyway. There's plenty of time."

"Okay, but I still don't think it's a good idea," Buck said. He climbed into his plane, shaking his head, and took off.

Jack and I got a ride into town and enjoyed walking the streets, sightseeing. Hammondsport was charming, but small. It didn't take long to take in the sights. Periodically, I asked Jack if we should be leaving, to which he answered, "Plenty of time. Plenty of time." Eventually, I stopped asking and relaxed. We strolled along the waterfront, where beautiful mahogany motorboats were docked.

"I got an idea. We don't have lakes in Kansas."

He walked up to a guy tying his wooden boat to the dock. Jack offered him a bill. The man nodded and untied his boat.

Jack motioned for me to come over. "Take off your boots. We're going for a ride, and you can't go for a boat ride in leather boots." We took off our footwear. Tossing them on the dock, we rolled up our pants. He helped me into the vessel. I wiggled my toes. It felt odd to have my feet exposed.

The craft glistened in the sunlight. "Do you know how to operate one of these?"

Jack grinned. "How hard can it be? It's just a small airplane engine with the propeller in the water instead of the air. No problem."

"I guess."

The owner pull-started the motor. "Here's the throttle. Remember to slow way down way before you get—"

Jack pushed the throttle all the way forward, and we were off. The motor pulled the back end of the boat down slightly, and we sped across the glassy surface of the lake. The warm sun and wind on my face and in my hair were exhilarating. He went straight out, then circled and made figure eights, bumping and shaking across our wake. Laughing at his antics, I held on for dear life. I heard his laughter over the wind and the motor, and then he turned it off. Drifting in the middle of the lake, we leaned back and relaxed.

Jack kissed me. "Having fun?"

"Always with you, but I don't want you to get in trouble."

"They can do without me for an afternoon," he said. He dozed in the sunshine, awakening half an hour later.

"I told the guy we wouldn't be out long. Here. You drive."

We switched seats, and I cruised around the lake. "What fun! I don't remember driving a boat before."

"Well, it's time you did."

The motor sputtered a bit, so we slowly headed back toward the dock. When he realized that we had enough gas to make it in, he took the pilot's seat, gradually speeding up until he was heading straight for the dock at full throttle. The owner stood yelling and waving at us. Jack throttled back at the last instant possible, causing a large wave to rush over us and shift the boat so that it floated parallel to the dock. The timing was perfect. The boat only lightly bumping against it. The owner shook his head and grabbed the side, then shook his head again and laughed. Jack tossed him the rope, which the owner secured to a post.

"Thanks, fella," Jack said as we picked up our boots and

walked toward a bench. The owner looked on, chuckling and shaking his head.

Back in town, we passed a shop with a dress in the window that I liked. "I feel gritty and windblown. I'm going to buy a change of clothes. How about we get a room in the hotel? It's really too late to fly back to Syracuse."

"Sounds good. You get the room. I need to go out to the airport to check the cargo and make sure it's okay. Meet you back at the hotel. We'll go get supper."

About midnight, Jack got out of bed and dressed. "Where are you going?"

"I'm going to the hangar to guard the cargo. I can't afford for some of the bottles to get stolen. I found a guy who will take me out there. He agreed to take you at six thirty in the morning. Okay?"

"I'll just go with you now. I'm awake. Won't Pang be mad?"

"Nah. I'll come up with something to distract him. We will really have to leave early in the morning, though."

Before we left the next morning, Jack turned to me. "I've come up with a plan to distract Pang. I'll land so that he can't see the whole plane. Don't get out until I'm talking with Pang, then you come in. There's a side door."

At the airfield in Syracuse, we taxied to the hangar. Buck motioned when it was safe for me to get out. I did as Jack said and entered the hangar by a side door, curious how he would get out of his predicament. Pang looked at me curiously, but didn't say anything. At the sight of Jack, Pang rushed over, face crimson, but Jack got in the first word.

"Hey, Pang. You a short snorter? Give me two bucks, will ya?" Jack said.

"What? Why?" Pang said, reaching for his wallet without question. With a just few words and a grin, Jack had diffused Pang's anger.

"I'll show you." Jack told Pang to sign the bills and hand them to him.

Pang did as he was told. Jack signed the bills with his name and the notation "Short Snorter #1," handing one of the bills back to Pang.

"Hey, give me my other bill," Pang exclaimed.

"You are now an official Short Snorter. I'm number one. You're number two. You get a buck a trick. Ain't that a good gag?" Jack said. He walked off, whistling.

"Damn you, Ashcraft," Pang yelled after him. "I'll get you back."

I met Jack and laughed. "You're so bad."

I didn't feel sorry for Pang for long, though. He cleaned house that night at the party.

I couldn't wait to pull it on the Skylarks.

CHAPTER 15
JACK LEAVES THE CIRCUS

ANXIOUSLY, I waited for the girls to arrive. I couldn't wait to have some fun with them with Jack's gag. When they finally arrived, I had them sit in three chairs I had lined up in front of my desk. They looked at me, puzzled, but did as I asked.

When they were seated, I leaned on my desk and said, "Give me two dollars apiece." I was prepared to supply the money if they didn't have any.

"I'm not sure I have two bills on me," Frances said.

"Same here," Viola laughed.

Ruth produced two. "What's this about?"

"I'll show you in a bit," I said.

After several minutes digging in pockets and purses, Frances and Viola produced two very crumpled bills each. "Okay, sign them and give them to me."

Growing more curious, they complied, one by one. I signed the bills with my name, followed by "Short Snorter #1," and handed each of them back one of their bills.

"Now you're a Short Snorter," I said.

"Hey, where's my other dollar bill?" Frances protested.

"Yeah, I work hard for my money," Viola said.

"Suckers. Texas Guinan would be proud," I said, and they laughed. "It's a practical joke that Jack thought up to get out of trouble. I couldn't wait to pull it on you, but I'll be glad to give you your money back."

"I'll take mine back," Viola said. "I'll be able to make a quick buck off this. See you next time."

"Before you go," Ruth said, "I want to tell you what an amazing landing Mavis made outside of Baltimore, coming back from Fredericksburg. We got caught in a terrible thunderstorm and had to make an emergency landing in a really small field outside of town. To be honest, I didn't even think her odds of pulling off the landing were fifty-fifty, but she did it."

Ruth's words brought tears to my eyes as I remembered that horrible night and how close we came to crashing. "Thanks, Ruth. That was a real test. It gave me confidence to have you with me. I don't know if I would have put our odds that high, but we made it."

"Here's to Mavis," they all said, holding up imaginary wine glasses.

"See you at the field," Viola said.

Frances looked at me. "Okay, gal. Tell us the rest of the story."

"What do you mean?"

"You know what she means," Ruth said. "Why did Jack come up with the gag? What trouble did he need to get out of? There's something you're not telling us."

I laughed. "You know me too well." I told them about our side trip to Hammondsport for the bubbly and how we got sidetracked by exploring the town and the boat ride.

"I can't tell you how much fun I have with Jack. He gets me to do things I can't even imagine. Mother and Daddy would be aghast. Well, at least Mother would."

"I'm envious in a way," Frances said, "but I have met this certain instructor . . ."

"Oh, yeah?" I said, but she clammed up.

"Don't be envious," I said. "Our relationship has nowhere to go. He's a vagabond of the sky. His schedule would never permit it. Mother and Daddy would never accept him because of what they see as our position in society. I have so much fun with him, but I love running a newspaper."

"Then just have fun while it lasts," Ruth said.

"I will, but my heart will break when it comes time to say goodbye."

Nineteen twenty-six closed out about like '25 did, except there was no attack on New York City. Jack and I went to the Macy's parade again, but then he had to help with preparations to head south after the first of the year. Their planes and their engines needed overhauled to even get to Florida.

There was the usual flurry of parties. There was one gathering in particular where someone caught my interest.

Sitting alone at a table in the shadows of a column sipping sherry, I contemplated whether to stay or not. A quick survey of the room revealed the usual partygoers. Ruth made the social rounds as well, but she was married to flying. There was one man I couldn't remember seeing before. He was tall, with dark hair combed back. Quite handsome, actually. He walked smoothly and confidently across the room, stopping occasionally to talk to someone. He glanced my way, then started talking to a particular woman, so I didn't give him a second thought. Slowly, I stirred my drink, deciding to leave when it was gone.

"Excuse me. Are you Mavis Perkins?"

I hadn't seen anyone walk in my direction, and I turned quickly to see who had spoken, spilling my drink.

"I'm so sorry," a man said, pulling his handkerchief from his pocket to clean up the liquid.

I grabbed a napkin. "I am. Who wants to know?"

Blue eyes with dark edges looked into mine and lingered for a few moments. I guess I was a sucker for blue eyes. There stood the man I had noticed earlier.

"I am so sorry. May I introduce myself," he said, standing tall. "My name is Reese Bennett Carrington III." He smiled. "Reese to my friends. Never Benny—I left that behind when I was ten. Your friend told me that we should meet." He motioned with his head in Ruth's direction. She smiled impishly and wiggled her fingers at me.

"Oh, she did, did she? How can I help you?"

"Ruth told me that you are a pilot. I am as well. I thought we could do some hangar flying."

I laughed. "Ruth is the aviator. I fly a plane when I get the chance. Daddy lets me fly his Waco, but I do so recreationally. How about you?"

"I fly often for various reasons, but that's not my end goal. In their own way, outfits like flying circuses remind people that flying is here to stay. This is just the beginning for aviation," he said, then paused.

"Please, continue."

"Planes like theirs are getting obsolete. The new regulations will eventually shut them down. It's also just a matter of time before someone hops the pond," he said.

"What does this all have to do with you?" I asked.

"I want to start an airline," he said. "I predict that we will see rapid developments in aircraft in the next few years. Designs will improve. Engines will get more powerful and be more durable and faster. I have a partner. We want to be ready when all this happens."

We talked for an hour, and then he escorted me home. Reese was very charming. He asked to see me again.

In early February, Jack called me.

"Hi, Mavis," Jack said. "Florida's a bust. Daws couldn't get us appearances down there. Ed said the same, but lots is happening here. Can you meet me at Josie's this evening? Say, at seven?"

I was glad that he'd called before I had left for home. Tired of the commute to and from the city, I'd decided to find a place on Long Island, but hadn't identified where. I would miss Gerald, but not the commute.

At Josie's, Jack rushed in, ordered a hamburger, and got right to the point.

"Like I said, Florida was a bust. Gates talked to some Department of Commerce guys about the new regulations."

"I've been hearing about them as well. Go on."

"Gates was steamed when they told him that our planes are getting old and unsafe. Truth is, they're right. Our planes wouldn't even make it to Florida if we wanted to go, but Gates is stubborn and wants to prove them wrong. So they rented some old warehouses in Teterboro as headquarters. We're going to completely redo the planes." He paused to take giant bites of his hamburger. "We'll go to shows from there, then come back. Pennsylvania and New York are the most profitable for us, anyway."

"My, that is a lot of news," I said. It would certainly be easier for us to meet, but I wasn't sure where our relationship would go with Reese in the picture.

"They will have headquarters to operate out of, so that will be easier on the guys. They're changing the name to Gates Flying Service," Jack said between bites, slowing down as he became satiated. "We'll do other things like give lessons and even design and manufacture airplanes."

"My, that is interesting news."

"That's not all," he said, and took a deep breath. "I'm leaving the circus."

"You're what?"

"I've decided to leave the circus and head out on my own," he said. "See what Jack Ashcraft can do. Buck and Babcock are going with me."

"How did this all come about?"

"I've made a lot of contacts the last couple of years. I met this guy named Bert Crader in Towanda, Pennsylvania. He said that they are keen to get an airport there and want me and Buck to help them, so that will be our summer headquarters. Our buddy Gardner Nagle from Shreveport is going in on it with us. Get this! They are even buying us new airplanes. Wacos," he said, grinning.

"I'm overwhelmed with all this news. When will all of this happen?"

"Soon. It's still a little cold to fly much, so I'm going to help with the overhaul of the planes to make sure they're ready to go and make plans. I'll head for Towanda in the spring. Gates is putting on his own air show this fall. Buck's flying in it. I'm making other plans. I'll probably fly in the National Air Race this year from New York to Spokane."

"I see."

"I don't know what this means for us. I'll be closer for a

while, but I will be busier than ever before, and then I'll leave. Who knows when I'll be back in town."

"It's okay," I said softly. "I've met someone . . ."

Jack looked surprised, a little hurt, then relieved. "I'm happy for you, Mavis. I really am. I hope he deserves you."

CHAPTER 16
RACES AND FLYING THE POND

JUST AS REESE HAD PREDICTED, aviation was rapidly advancing, and Roosevelt Field was at the center of things. Rumors were abundant and rampant. The biggest was who would be the first to fly across the Atlantic. A hotel guy named Raymond Orteig had offered a large prize for the first to do so. In May, I received word that Admiral Byrd and others were gathering at Roosevelt Field as the takeoff point to cross the Atlantic. I rushed to the fields to see what was happening. Planes were scattered on the field, their pilots nearby. I got out my notepad and got to work.

Jack was there and ran over. "I had a student up for a lesson and saw a bunch of people here, so I landed pronto to come check it out."

"Everyone's after Orteig's prize money for being the first to fly across the Atlantic," I said. "It's all about races and records now."

"Twenty-five thousand dollars is a good incentive, I guess, but having nothing but water under me for thirty hours, or worse, is not for me."

"Me neither, but more power to them."

"Byrd and his crew are here as well as others—some names I don't recognize," I said, showing him my list. "Women want to fly across the Atlantic too. I've heard of a couple. One is Ruth Elder. I heard she's here checking things out. Everybody's waiting for the weather to clear."

Ruth and Frances showed up to watch the action.

As we walked and talked, a plane we didn't recognize circled the field and landed. The pilot, tall and slender, alighted. *Spirit of St. Louis* was painted on the nose.

"Hey, I know that guy. That's Charles Lindbergh," Jack exclaimed. "Our paths crossed out west. Come on, I'll introduce you."

"Hey, Slim," Jack called out as we approached. "So, you're going to try to hop across the pond, huh?"

"That's the plan," Lindbergh replied.

"What's your plane? How do you see out of the thing without side windows?"

I had wondered the same thing, but was afraid to ask for fear I would sound ignorant.

"It's a Ryan. Custom made for me. I have a periscope and a compass. That's all I really need over water," Lindbergh said.

"I guess. I like seeing where I'm going. This is Mavis Perkins. She owns a newspaper here on the island."

I chatted with Lindbergh while Jack examined his plane.

"How much fuel you going to take?" Jack asked.

"Just enough."

"Well, I reckon if anybody can make it across the Atlantic, you can. Good luck, buddy," Jack said, shaking his hand.

Others started crowding around Lindbergh, so Jack and I moved on.

Frances, Ruth, and Viola were there and ran over to say hello.

"Lindbergh, right? This is all so exciting," Ruth said. "I'm envious. I would love to fly across the ocean."

"You're braver than I am," I answered.

Frances pulled at Ruth's arm. "Not me! Come on! I've heard Ruth Elder is here checking things out. Let's go find her. See you later!"

"If you see her, invite her to our meeting."

They waved in acknowledgement.

"I have more news if you have time," Jack said.

The crowd dwindled at the airfield and activity subsided, so Jack and I decided to have a quick lunch. We settled in the booth at Josie's and ordered sandwiches.

"Here's the plan," he started. "September 2, I'm going to Elmira to fly in an air meet to open the new airport. Jimmy Doolittle is going to be there. As a flier, it's always good to have your name on the same bill as Doolittle. He's only giving a demonstration, but that's still good."

"I've heard he's amazing."

Jack nodded. "After that, I'm flying in the National Air Race, like I said. We start out of Roosevelt Field and fly to Spokane. It'll be my first long-distance race. I'm really excited about it."

"How wonderful! When is that?"

"We take off September 21—weather permitting, that is."

"If possible, I'll be here to cheer you on. Will you fly solo?"

Jack shook his head. "Bert's flying as observer and navigator. After the races, we'll do some flying in upstate New York, and on the way to Macon, Georgia, where we'll set up winter headquarters. My brother Franz will come to join us there."

"All this takes my breath away. I'm so excited for you, Jack. It will be fun for you to fly with your brother. How old is he?"

"He's only twenty-two. He's begged me for two years to let him come fly with me. I'm not sure this is the life for him, but I can't put him off any longer."

"Hopefully it will all work out."

"I hope so."

Three days later, Frances called me early. "Lindbergh's tired of waiting. He's getting ready to take off. Better get down here if you want to see it."

I called Jack while I dressed, then I was off to Roosevelt. A few hundred people had already arrived to see Lindbergh take off. Reese was at the periphery with a group, his back to me. He hadn't spotted me. Officials were milling around a particular hangar.

Jack rushed up. "Have I missed anything?"

"No, but he's definitely taking off," I said, pointing. "He said that he was tired of waiting for the weather to improve."

"He'll probably fly out of it."

I nodded. "Like he said, he has his compass."

"And his altimeter," Jack added. "The toughest thing will be staying awake and alert that long. He probably didn't sleep much last night."

Roustabouts attached The *Spirit of St. Louis* to a truck, which towed it into position with a car leading the way. There were photographs taken with officials, his mother, and another pilot. Lindbergh then put on his flight coveralls and got ready to take off. The runway was muddy, and the aircraft, laden with 450 gallons of fuel, managed to move forward. Slowly, it gathered speed, bouncing as it struggled to become airborne. The plane lifted from the runway, barely clearing the high line wires by twenty feet at the edge of the field. Slowly, the aircraft disappeared into the mist like a spirit, which I thought befitting its name. Official takeoff time was 7:52 a.m.

Jack watched wistfully. "Godspeed, my friend."

I tugged at Jack's sleeve to get his attention. "Bye, Jack. I've got to go. Keep in touch."

He glanced over at me. "Sure thing," he said, then looked back at the sky where he'd last seen Lindbergh's plane.

I went to find Reese. Anxiously, we—New York, the United States, and the rest of the world—awaited word of Lindbergh. That night, we received word that he had landed in Paris thirty-three hours and thirty minutes after taking off. Tens of thousands of people had greeted him.

Ruth Elder was indeed at the airport the day Lindbergh left. She took time to join us for the meeting of the Snooty Skylarks on Sunday. Ruth laughed when she read her official membership card that I prepared for her. She was twenty-five but looked younger.

"I'm a journalist, so I'm going to ask you what I ask every pilot I meet," I told her.

She smiled. "Ask away."

"How did you start flying?"

"My husband. He taught me to fly. We were living in Florida at the time. I saw it as a way out. I entered beauty pageants to pay for lessons."

"A way out of what?" I asked.

"I was born in Alabama. We were as poor as church mice. I saw opportunities for myself in flying that I never saw before. Then some businessmen approached me about flying the Atlantic."

"Why do you want to do that? It sounds pretty dangerous, if you ask me."

Ruth thought for a few moments before she replied. "The way I see it, I'll make it across, or I won't. Worst thing that will happen is that I'll die trying and die satisfied that I tried. If I do make it across, I'll be famous and make more in a week than I would in five years in Alabama." She paused and laughed. "And I've always dreamed of owning a Paris gown."

We all laughed, but we seriously thought about what she had said.

"George Haldeman will be the main pilot. He's a fantastic pilot and will do most of the flying. I will smile and bring in the sponsors. To me, it's worth the risk."

"Are you afraid?" Ruth Nichols asked.

Ruth Elder looked at each one of us. "Maybe a little, but we can't let fear stop us from doing anything, can we? Especially flying."

We all shook our heads.

"I have to go now," Ruth Elder said.

I nodded. "I have one request. If you live to tell about it, please come back and give us the scoop, okay? What is said between us stays between us."

She nodded, gave each of us a quick hug, and walked out the door. Viola had to leave as well.

After she left, Ruth and Frances asked how things were with Jack.

"He's leaving the circus to go out on his own."

"That's an interesting turn of events," Frances said.

"He and Buck are setting up headquarters in Towanda, Pennsylvania. The city even bought them new Wacos.

Jack's going to represent them in the National Air Races in September."

"Tough to carry on a romance with him on the go all the time," Ruth said.

"I agree. I love the man, but I just don't see a future." I looked at Ruth. "Reese and I have been on a few dates. He's such a gentleman. I've told Jack about him."

They both raised their eyebrows.

June 13, Jack and I met at the ticker tape parade for Lindbergh. The city gave the aviator a hero's welcome. Officials estimated four million people greeted him. An unknown number dropped tons of paper tape from stock tickets from windows above the street. I was enjoying the parade when Jack saw someone he knew, then just disappeared. Reese had told me that he would be at the parade and where he would be, so I headed there to find him.

Late June, I was back at Roosevelt with Reese. We were there to see Reese's flying friend, Admiral Richard Byrd, take off to fly the Atlantic. We'd heard rumors of discord, but Byrd had a crew with him—Floyd Bennett, Bernt Balchen, Bert Acosta, and George Noville. Byrd hadn't decided who would actually be pilot.

Yes, indeed. Aviation was advancing rapidly.

CHAPTER 17
THE BIG RACE

NINETEEN TWENTY-SEVEN STARTED busy and stayed that way. Ruth Nichols earned her transport license in September, so that was cause for celebration. From late summer on, it seemed I was at the airfields constantly, covering the news. Thankfully, I had found an appropriate place to live on the island. September rolled around, and I thought about Jack flying in the meet in Elmira. I was able to get a copy of the newspaper to read about it. Doolittle's flying was tremendous and made the headlines, but Jack flew well himself. There was an article.

The New York to Spokane National Air Race was scheduled to start September 21. Jack sent word that he would fly to Roosevelt the weekend before to prepare. On my way to the office Monday morning, I went by the airfield. There he was with his new Waco. He and another guy were walking around the aircraft, examining every inch.

"Cowboy Jack!" I said, rushing over. He gave me a quick hug and kissed me on the cheek.

"It's so good to see you! This is your new ship, huh?" I said, admiring the airplane.

"She's a beauty, isn't she?"

"Indeed she is. What's this about?" I asked, pointing to the name painted on the nose. "The *Spirit of Ammonia?*"

He smiled. "Me and Buck wanted to have fun with the *Spirit of St. Louis*. Buck named his the *Spirit of Camphor*. We didn't think Lindbergh would mind."

I laughed. "I hope not."

The other man walked up and looked at me, then at Jack.

"Bert, I want you to meet a good friend of mine, Mavis Perkins. She owns a newspaper here on the island."

"Nice to meet you, ma'am, but I'm trying to keep Jack focused," he said. He turned to Jack. "But he keeps getting distracted, especially with all the pretty women around."

"Relax, will you, Bert?" Jack said. "We don't take off until Wednesday, if the fog lifts. We've been over the maps and charts and examined the damn plane so many times that its tired of us looking at it."

"I just want to make sure everything is ready, that's all."

"I appreciate it, Bert, but we'll be fine," Jack said. "You even told that other reporter that I'm the best fog pilot in the business."

Bert held up his hands. "Okay, okay."

"Speaking of pretty women," I said, "I saw Ruth Elder on my way in. Here she is now."

"Hey, Mavis," Ruth called, and ran over. "What are you doing here?"

"Hi, Ruth. I'd like for you to meet a friend of mine, Jack Ashcraft. Big Jack, Cowboy Aviator in the newspapers. Jack, this is Ruth Elder."

Jack nodded to Ruth. "Nice to meet you, ma'am. I read that you're planning to fly across the pond?"

"Sure am. George Haldeman will be the main pilot.

He's the best. We're just waiting for the weather to clear up some."

"Still seems mighty risky to me, but why not try? If you're successful, you'll get more offers than you'll know what to do with."

Ruth nodded. "That's what I'm hoping for. I was getting nowhere in Alabama and Florida, that's for sure."

"Let me get a picture of you two," I said. While I was adjusting my camera, Jack picked Ruth up and placed her in the middle of the propellor and held it level. The propeller looked like a legless bench and made for a great photo.

Walking off the field, we saw a group of four boys about twelve years old. One waved, and then to my surprise, he ran over. "Hey, Mr. Jack! Remember me?" The others followed.

"I believe I do. How are you doing, Billy? You still throwing those homemade planes at people?"

For the next several minutes, I ceased to exist as far as they were concerned.

"Oh, no, sir. My dad broke me of doing that. I read in the newspaper that you were flying in that race to Spokane, Washington?"

"Yes, sir, I am. We're scheduled to take off Wednesday if the weather's good."

"Hot dang," he said. "I might have to play hooky from school to watch you."

Jack laughed. "I can't encourage that, but I wouldn't tell on you if you did."

All the while, the other three boys watched and listened, starstruck and impressed that their friend knew Jack.

"There's one place you can come to if you can make it

out there," Jack said, "and that's Teterboro. Gates has set up shop there."

"Hot dang! Will you be there?"

"I'll be in and out, but there will always be pilots around."

"I'll be there, then. These are my buddies," Billy said, and Jack shook hands with them. Shyly, they each said, "Nice to meet you, sir."

Then Jack introduced me. "This is my friend Mavis Perkins. She owns a newspaper here on Long Island. She's a pilot too."

The boys seemed surprised but politely said that it was nice to meet me.

"Excuse us. We've got to go now. Bye!" Billy said, and the boys walked off.

I heard one of the boys say, "I can't believe you know Big Jack."

Another said, "Can you believe that girl is a pilot?"

"My, you have interesting fans," I said.

"Everywhere we go, there are the kids. We don't mind, because we've got to bring up the next generation of pilots. We get them to do odd jobs for us and play practical jokes on them."

Very early Wednesday morning, I headed over to the airfield. Racers were making final preparations. For two days, the weather had been poor. Rain and fog lingered over Roosevelt Field and all of Long Island. The field was a sloppy mess. Officials and airmen debated whether to let the airplanes take off or not. For a brief moment, the sun broke through the clouds, but it was quickly obscured again. Everyone took it as an omen to start the race. It was my opinion that they should take off, because the weather wasn't going to get better in the foreseeable future, and they would probably fly out of the clouds as they moved east. They had compasses and altimeters.

To my surprise, Reese was there to observe the activity. "Hello, Mavis," he said, and kissed me on the cheek. "You know someone flying in the race?"

"Yes. My friend Jack Ashcraft and Bert Crader are flying in a Waco. The city of Towanda, Pennsylvania is sponsoring them."

"I saw his name on the roster."

We heard the roar of engines. One by one, chocks were pulled and airplanes taxied down the runway and took off. Jack and Bert were last to take off.

Jack was a safe pilot, but there were so many things that could go wrong—bad weather, the cold, fog concealing the peaks of mountains, engine trouble.

Godspeed, my friend.

Reese and I went for coffee and breakfast to warm up.

A week and a half later, Jack sent me the front page of the *Spokane Daily Chronicle*, which listed the placing of the racers. He and Bert had placed seventh. He included a short note that said that it was cold as hell halfway there when skies finally cleared. They would have placed better but had magneto problems and had to turn back.

Jack went on to say that he was stopping by Kansas to see his parents on the way to Georgia. One of his sisters had died unexpectedly earlier that year.

. . .

Less than a month had passed when we heard of another attempted crossing of the Atlantic. This time, it was Ruth Elder and her pilot George Haldeman. They were to take off October 11. The Skylarks barely had time to get to the airfield in time to see the *American Girl* take to the skies. We couldn't believe that someone we knew, one of us, was actually attempting such a daring flight.

Ruth looked on longingly. "I'm so envious."

Once it was in the skies, all we could do was anxiously wait.

Time enough for them to arrive at their destination came and went, and still no word. Our hearts fell, and we feared the worst. Then on October 13, authorities received word that an oil line had burst and they had gone down at sea. To their good fortune, they were rescued by a Dutch oil tanker nearby. Although they hadn't made it to their destination, Ruth had flown farther than any woman had flown before—2,623 miles, and just 360 miles short of land. The Parisians were elated to celebrate Ruth's failure with her.

When she returned to the United States two weeks later, it seemed all of America wanted to as well. Everyone wanted a piece of her and some of her time, but she stole away to be with the Snooty Skylarks for a few minutes. She disguised herself as a roustabout in men's coveralls and snuck into a taxi. We met at the newspaper office. Quickly, I opened and closed the door.

"Did anyone see you leave?" I asked, looking out the window.

"I don't think so."

I turned to her and laughed. "So, you were feted in Paris, greeted by fireboats when you arrived back in New York. Then you met the President at the White House and had a ticker tape parade!"

"And I failed in my attempt!" Ruth laughed, accepting the glass of champagne I offered her.

"I heard you got offered four hundred thousand dollars for your story," Frances said.

"I've heard that as well, but what I did get is more gowns in Paris than I'll ever wear, if anyone wants one. I've never owned two dresses at one time!"

Ruth Nichols listened and seemed to be plotting something in her mind. "Tell us about the actual flight."

"It was rough. George did most of the flying, but it was rough the whole way. The storms were terrible. He needed a break sometimes. I could hardly control the plane. We had finally gotten through the rough part and were feeling good about our prospects when the oil line broke. We knew we were doomed then. We were darned lucky the oil tanker was nearby. Those guys were so sweet. They treated us great."

"What's next for you?"

"I signed a contract for vaudeville. I've had movie people contact me as well. That will be interesting. I don't think all this fame will last long, but it'll be fun while it lasts. I've seen and done more than I could ever have dreamed of."

"Yes, fame is fleeting," Ruth Nichols said, "but you always have us."

We all raised our glasses in a toast to women fliers and bade our friend and sister farewell. I wondered when or if I would see Ruth Elder again.

REESE and I made the rounds at the never-ending number of cocktail parties over the holidays. With each passing day, my feelings for him grew stronger. The feeling was mutual. Over the few short months that we had known one another, I thought less about Jack and more about him. Mother approved, despite the fact he was a pilot. Not that I felt I needed their approval, but peace in the family was good. I told him about Jack.

Reese and I rang in the new year together. Waiting for him to get out of bed, I was enjoying my morning coffee and reading a newspaper. To my surprise, below the crease, there was photograph of Ruth and a short article on the front page. I sat up straight in my chair. The article stated that the Flying Debutante aviatrix Ruth Nichols and Harry Rogers were planning a flight from Rockaway Beach, Queens, in an attempt to set a speed record from New York to Miami. The article had few details about the flight and who had arranged it. Having a beautiful woman as a pilot made for good press and publicity. They would take off January 4. The article didn't explicitly say so, but the timing was specific and perfect. The flight coincided with a convention of newspaper editors in Miami.

I had no doubt that Ruth would be successful. The next day, I sent her a telegraph at the Royal Palm Hotel to congratulate her. The Skylarks would be anxious to hear about the flight and would meet over the weekend if she was available. Two weeks later, we were able to meet.

She rushed in, excited and out of breath. "I've had the most amazing two weeks! You won't believe all that's happened."

"We're waiting."

"Let's see. Where do I start? After we talked with Ruth Elder, I was feeling a little down, wondering what I was going to do next. A new year was coming up, and I had no prospects on the horizon. Then late last week I got a call from Harry."

"Harry, the nincompoop guy."

"Yes, the nincompoop guy," Ruth said. "I always thought he was teasing."

"I saw the article in the paper. I have to say that I was surprised."

"Me too. Harry wouldn't let me tell anyone. I didn't have time, anyway. He told me that he had a rich aviator friend, and they wanted to make a nonstop flight to Miami. They had been reading about Ruth and George and agreed that a woman pilot made headlines. Harry told his friend that he knew one with a seaplane license. Me. He asked me if I wanted to come along. I knew the route. I'd flown it twice with my aunt. Of course, he knew what my answer would be."

Frances looked on in disbelief. "That's amazing."

"No kidding. New Year's Day, I went to Rockaway Beach to see the plane. She was a beauty. Sherman

Fairchild with a heated cabin, single cockpit. Silver pontoons. Red fuselage with yellow wings. It carries four passengers, but he had extra fuel tanks put in."

"Mavis said that you took off January 4," Viola said.

"That's right. They had everything ready. It was chilly when we left. Wind out of the north, so a tailwind was nice. Sky was cloudless. It was beautiful, actually. The rising sun cast rainbow reflections on the water. At 7:55, Harry took off from Rockaway Beach. We changed places off the coast of Virginia. Harry had to jump quickly over the back of the seat without letting go of the stick until I slid into place from the other side and took hold of it."

We laughed, visualizing the exchange.

"I traveled light. All I took was a change of clothes and a dress for the party that night. The weather was good for the most part. We encountered a squall around Savannah, but that was easy to ride out. It was good to see the ice and snow disappear as we flew south."

"How high did you fly?" Frances asked.

"About twelve hundred feet," Ruth said. "The sunset over Daytona Beach was beautiful, but it was hard to fly after dark. Then we spotted bonfires they lit to guide us. We made a perfect landing in Miami. The flight was marvelous. The whole experience was amazing."

I imagined the scene. "The photographers were probably waiting for you. And the reporters. And the handlers."

"Were they ever. The photographers were aggressive about recording the moment. I saw spots for hours, but the reporters did their jobs and reported that Fairchild planes are safe. I told them that the cabin was so quiet that a businessman could dictate to his stenographer. They latched on to that as I hoped they would. As far as the spectators were concerned, you would have thought we had flown across the

Atlantic. The handlers got us where we needed to be. Fairchild was pleased, which was important."

"I assume Harry doesn't think you're a nincompoop anymore," I said.

"What's next?" Frances asked.

"It gets even better, if you can believe it. Fairchild offered me a job as 'flying salesgirl' and will pay me sixty dollars a week! Get this—they are even providing a Rearwin airplane for me to fly! I keep pinching myself to make sure I'm not dreaming. I'll be flying around the country setting up aviation clubs as well."

"Woohoo!" we all said.

"That definitely calls for some celebration," I said, opening the cabinet door for champagne.

"I don't know when you'll see me next," Ruth said.

"That's okay. Just drop us a note now and then or call. We'll meet when you're back in town."

Jack sent me a note that he and his brother Francis, whom he called Franz, had arrived in Macon. Enclosed was a photo of a young pilot leaning against an airplane, one leg casually crossed over the other. I imagined peach fuzz on his cheeks. Jack, Franz, Buck, Bert Crader, and a pilot named Gardner were working with city officials on plans for a huge air meet in February 1928. He listed some of the more famous pilots that he had lined up to appear. It was impressive.

By all appearances, all was going well with Cowboy Jack. He had a new life; I had mine. I thought of him less and less, but always fondly.

· · ·

On Sunday, February 18, I was preparing to leave to meet Reese for lunch when the phone rang.

Jack was on the other end of the line, hysterical. I could barely understand what he was saying. "Mavis. It was just awful, just awful," he cried. "Franz and Buck are dead. A bomb went off and killed them. I wanted to talk to someone. I didn't know who to call," he sobbed.

Then I heard someone in the background. "Gardner, take care of Jack, will you? I'll talk to Mavis."

"Let me talk to Mavis," Jack shouted.

"Settle down, Jack. It's okay. You can talk to her later, okay?"

I heard a scuffle, and then Bert got on the line. "Mavis, this is Bert."

"What's going on, Bert?" I demanded. "A bomb killed Franz and Buck? What in the world happened?"

"Buck and Franz went up to throw out loud fireworks to alert the public about the air show—you know, to bring people out to the airfield." Bert choked up and had to pause to regain his composure.

Several moments passed.

"Bert, you still there?"

"I'm still here. Gardner was up at the same time. He saw everything. All was going okay. Two of the bombs went off fine, then the third exploded early. It blew a wing off, there was an explosion, and the boys crashed. We're not sure what happened yet."

Horrified, I imagined the scene.

Again, Bert had to pause to regain his composure. "I feel awful. It was my idea, but we all agreed to it. We even practiced how it would go . . . I feel just awful."

I didn't try to hold back my tears when I heard of the

tragedy. Poor Jack. Desperately, I wanted to go to him, but I knew I couldn't. Neither did I have words for Bert.

"What's going to happen with Jack?" I asked. "He sounded like he's in bad shape."

"He is. He was in shock but holding it together. Then he called his parents. That's when he went to pieces," Bert said. "We're doing the best we can for him, but it's hard to know what to do. We're getting a doctor."

"I understand. Please keep me informed, okay?"

"I will. I called Pang. He's sending a couple of guys down to help. That will be good," Bert said. "Me and Gardner have to take care of some business here."

"That's good. Bye, Bert. I'm so sorry for all of you," I said. I hung up and tried to sort through all that I had heard. Distraught, I struggled to collect myself. Even though we had parted ways romantically, I still cared deeply for Jack.

Reese came to get me for lunch. I told him about the accident.

"That's awful. Are you okay?" he asked, and held me close, understanding my sorrow for a friend. He also knew of the triumphs and tragedies of being a pilot.

"I'm okay. I didn't know Jack's brother, but I saw a photo. He was so young. Only twenty-two. I just feel for him so much."

Pang called me Monday morning to update me on the situation. Neither Crader nor Gardner believed that Jack was up to flying, so Pang sent Ive and Al to help out. Pang had talked to Jack briefly. Jack insisted on appearing at the air meet in Endicott in May. In the meantime, Jack had to take his little brother home for burial. Al would accompany Jack to Kansas. Francis's death would devastate his parents and the family. Bert and Gardner would take care of unfinished business in Macon and go to Endicott; the others would wait at Teterboro for Jack's return.

Ed also called, and we met for coffee.

"Jack is sure having some tough luck lately, isn't he? Poor guy," he said.

"Did something else happen I didn't hear about?"

"You probably hadn't heard this," Ed continued, "but a guy named Grantland Irwin committed suicide by stepping off Jack's plane right before this happened."

"Oh my God."

"Yeah, and a sister died a year or so ago. The guy's been through a hell of a lot."

"He certainly has." I remembered Jack telling me it was Grantland's plane that he had borrowed for our weekend in Virginia. "His weekend home for Franz's funeral must have been hell for him," I said, tears in my eyes.

Fun-loving, happy prankster Jack was subdued when we finally met in early April. I hardly recognized him. He didn't seem like the same man. Gates had insisted that his pilots be clean-shaven, and that's the way I had always seen Jack, even after he left the circus, but that day he had several days' growth of stubble. He had lost weight, and his face was drawn, eyes reflecting the sorrow in his heart. Greeting him warmly, I kissed him on the cheek and led him to our table. I grasped his hands firmly.

I could tell that seeing me again was difficult for him, especially under the circumstances, so I gave him a few moments to collect himself before I spoke quietly.

"How are you doing?"

"Not good, but hanging in there," he whispered. "Going

home and facing Mother, Dad, and the family was the worst time in my life." Tears welled in his eyes and trickled down his once tanned face, which was now pale from what he had endured. Quickly, he pulled a handkerchief from his pocket and dried them. He looked around to see if anyone had noticed.

"You're safe with me, Jack."

Jack nodded. "I know. I've always appreciated that. That's why I'm here."

"Pang said that you are headed to Endicott for an air meet. Is that right?" I asked.

He nodded.

"My God, Jack. It's only been a few weeks since the crash. Can't you postpone it or something?" I asked.

"A commitment's a commitment," he said. "The guys at Endicott understand and have been great. Bert and Gardner have almost everything worked out. Jimmy Scott will lend a hand too. He's been my mechanic for a couple of years now. He's been a good friend, too. Ed said that he would come up and help out. We'll be okay."

"It still seems too soon to me."

"There's no good time," Jack said. "Truth of the matter is, I have to. Some don't know this, but the city seized a lot of our assets after the crash. I had to beg them to let me keep my plane so that I could earn a living."

"Oh my gosh. Can I help you?"

"I'm okay. My part of the proceeds from Endicott will help a lot. I'm managing an air show in Cortland right after Endicott, so I should be okay. I'm flying in Elmira too. Thanks for the offer, though. I really appreciate it."

"The offer stands. What's after Cortland and Elmira?"

"I don't rightly know. Me, Ive, and Bill will probably do some small shows on our own. After that, I think I'll head back to Teterboro. Pang said that I always had a job with them. I need some stability and time to think things through."

Pang called the day before the air meet in Endicott.

"Mavis—me, Bill, Ed, and Ive are going to Endicott to give Jack some moral support. We have an extra cockpit if you're interested in joining us. It'll be a short hop and back in one day."

"What time do I need to be there?"

The next morning, I arrived as they were doing final checks on their planes. We all climbed in for the two-and-a-half-hour flight to Endicott. When we arrived, I scrambled out to find Jack and let him know that we were there while the guys secured the planes.

I spotted his broad shoulders as he stood talking to someone. "Cowboy Jack!"

Jack spun on his heel and ran to me. He gave me a warm hug, which I returned. "Look who let me tag along with them. We all wanted to give you some moral support."

"Thanks, guys, that means a lot," he said. He gave the guys hugs like men do, by shaking hands and bumping shoulders.

"I've got to go now, but I'll see you when I'm back on the ground," he said, smiling. "This is Gardner. Take care of Mavis, will you? Whoever those blokes are, they can fend for themselves."

Jack then pulled me aside to show me two photos, one of Franz and one of Buck. "I'm dedicating this flight to them," he said, pocketing the pictures.

Jack pulled out the ticket from our flight in Philadelphia. "If you can stay a little longer, I'll take you on a flight that will take your breath away. I'll personally see to it that you get home."

Not sure what I wanted to do, I slowly took the ticket from him.

For those fortunate enough to be at the air show that day, Jack gave the exhibition of his lifetime. All of us stood and watched, mesmerized, as did the spectators. We marveled at the artistry of the performance.

"I've never seen Jack fly like this," Ive said.

"Me neither," Ed joined in. "It's as if he's inspired."

"He is," I said. "He told me that he was dedicating the flight to Franz and Buck."

"Dang you, woman," Gardner said, and pulled his handkerchief from his pocket. When they thought no one was looking, the other guys quickly dried their eyes.

After the flight, Jack walked through the crowd, people clamoring to touch him and ask questions. He acknowledged them and was polite to everyone, but I could see the strain on his face.

I turned to Ed. "I'm going to say goodbye to Jack. I'll be there soon." Ed nodded, and I walked to Jack's office.

In his workspace, Jack leaned against the door to collect himself.

"That was an amazing performance, Jack," I said, stepping from the shadows.

"Mavis!" he said. "Don't you need to get back?"

"They'll wait a few minutes."

He took me in his arms and kissed me passionately. My emotions were in turmoil.

Then he gently pushed me away. "This isn't right. You're in love with someone else."

"I wanted to say goodbye. Take care of yourself, and I do hope things start going your way. You deserve it."

"Goodbye, Mavis. And thanks for coming. I really appreciate it. Tell the guys for me."

"I will." I handed him the ticket. "This is yours till next time. Call me for coffee when you're heading through town," I said, then turned and walked away.

The next day, I learned that Jack had won the stunt flying competition both days. The newspaper reported that the Texas Cowboy Aviator was awarded the Moose Trophy for his efforts.

THE SNOOTY SKYLARKS met when I returned to Long Island. Ruth was back in town for a few days, but Viola was gone, and no one knew where she had gone. I told the girls the news about Jack's brother and Buck getting killed in Georgia. "It was a particularly horrendous crash."

"Wow. That's a tough break," Frances exclaimed. "I remember reading about him and seeing his picture. It's easier to hear news like this when they are complete strangers."

Ruth nodded. "How's Jack getting along?"

"It's been rough for him, as you would expect. Pang sent Ive and Brooks to Macon to help. Gardner and Bert got him a doctor for his nerves. He probably had to be sedated to get some rest, but I'm just guessing. Pang said taking his brother's body back home and facing his parents was particularly difficult for him. Al traveled with him to Kansas. His little brother had just joined him in Macon."

No one spoke for a time as we contemplated the crash and how such events affect so many involved.

"Jack's back in the cockpit now. As he had planned, he

flew in the Endicott Air Meet in May and won a trophy. They say you can't let such things ground you, but God, it must've been difficult. Pang invited me to fly up with a few of them to offer moral support. His flying was amazing."

Again, we fell silent, contemplating. The only sound was the ticking of my clock.

"There are so many intersections in the aviation world," I said. "Triumph and tragedy. While the heartbreak of the crash in Macon unfolded, Amelia Earhart flew across the Atlantic as a passenger with Wilmer Stultz, Jack's colleague, as pilot."

"I remember Stultz from Jack's birthday party when he poured us a short snort of that nasty scotch," Frances said. "I hope he was sober when they took off. At least there was Louis Gordon, who could fly if need be."

"Amelia's moved to Rye to write about the crossing, and we've become good friends," Ruth said. "We wondered if there would be interest in a group of female fliers that advocated for women in aviation. I've met other gals in my travels around the country, including Louise Thaden. She's interested. She was amused when I told her about the Snooty Skylarks."

"I would love to have her as a member," I said.

"I just remembered something. On an earlier trip to Boston, I saw a seaplane in the harbor that was quite striking. It was orange with golden wings. As it turned out, it was Amelia's."

In early June, the plane was flown to Trepessey, Newfoundland. The three took off from there on June 18 to cross the Atlantic. They didn't make it to England or France but had to land near Wales, where they attached their plane to a buoy until they were discovered hours later.

When Amelia arrived home, there were great celebrations in Boston and Medford, Massachusetts, where she worked. Publisher G. P. Putnam of Rye, New York, and a guy named Railey had arranged for the flight.

At a later meeting, Ruth invited Amelia.

"You don't seem very excited," Frances said when she told us about the flight.

"I'm not. Stultz did all the flying. I didn't touch the controls, as I was promised," Amelia said. "The guys got paid. I didn't. What's to be excited about?"

"Stultz flew the whole time?" I asked.

"All of it. I was just a piece of baggage. A sack of potatoes."

"Why so much focus on you, then?" Frances asked.

"Because I was the first woman who actually crossed the ocean in an airplane. That's all. It's really kind of embarrassing. Some have even called me 'Lady Lindy.' I like Charles, but that is insulting to both of us. He probably doesn't like it one bit either. Maybe the publicity and the book will help me keep flying."

"Maybe it will help all women," Ruth said.

"So, you are the Snooty Skylarks Ruth told me about? Do *you* think there could be a bigger official organization?" Amelia said.

"Definitely." I handed Amelia her Snooty Skylarks card.

She looked at the card and laughed.

"I came up with Snooty Skylarks because some of the guys at the airfields call us snooty, but most are good guys. A women's organization is possible, but it will take some concerted effort, and frankly, after your excursion across the pond, your name will need to be associated with it."

.   .   .

Jack came through town, going somewhere, and wanted to meet for lunch, so we met at Josie's. It was good to see him. He looked healthier, and his spirits had improved.

"You're looking better."

"I'm feeling a little better. I really am, except I still have nightmares sometimes."

When we sat down, I noticed that his arms were bandaged.

Alarmed, I looked him in the eye, but he looked away. "What's this about?"

"I got my arms burned."

"Come on. You don't just tell me you got your arms burned. How?"

"Well, we were stopped at this dinky airfield in Rhode Island for gas, watching this guy doing some tame flying and stunting, when suddenly the tail went down. The plane crashed and burst into flames. I rushed over to try to save the poor fellas, but the fire was too intense. The police pulled me back."

"Jack! That's just like you. You could've been killed!" I couldn't hold back my emotions. "I swear. Your life is just so . . . crazy! You seem to attract bad luck sometimes."

He looked down sheepishly. "I know. It's kind of the nature of flying, but I've sure had a bad run here lately. The guys that pulled me away said that I kept screaming to Franz that I would save him."

"Jack, I'm so sorry."

"That's okay. I guess I'll be dealing with that for a while."

"Understandably so."

"Sad thing is, I found out later one of the guys was with

that Lafayette flying group in France and the other with the army flying corps during the war. They survived battles in France only to get killed in a crash in a dinky airfield in the US. That stinks."

"Sure does."

We talked for over an hour, reminiscing about the good times.

"Are you still flying?"

"I am." I told him about my landing in the storm in Virginia.

"Good for you! I'm proud of you."

"Thanks. Just having Ruth in the front cockpit helped a lot. She instructed me with simple hand motions. I don't know if I would have made it otherwise." I smiled. "Maybe a little of Jack was there too."

He returned my smile.

"I have to say, I was pleased, but more relieved. Ruth said I did a good job. That meant a lot to me and gave me a lot of confidence." Then I laughed. "No way I'm ever playing a bugle while landing, though."

"That's my schtick anyway."

Later in the year, Jack called to tell me that he had rejoined Gates as he'd said he would. He laughed and told me that for some reason, he'd tied his plane to the fence when he got to Teterboro.

I told him that Cowboy Jack had tied his steed to the corral. We agreed that it would be easier for us to get together for coffee with him in New Jersey.

Late fall, Jack called to tell me that he and three of the guys were leaving for one last tour of the Gates Flying Circus.

"Gates never had an official final tour and final show, so we're going to do this," he said.

Gates and Pang allowed Jack, Ive McKinney, Bill Brooks, and Homer Fackler to go up as pilots and take a couple of roustabouts and a couple of stuntmen with them. They'd had good luck in the South in the past and thought there would be few regulators there.

My thoughts were that the people down there were still recovering from the Mississippi River flood of 1927, and business wouldn't be good. Texaco had canceled their contract, so they would be on their own. Plus, there would be pilots out there with modern planes. However, I wished them well.

The group was gone only a few weeks when they wired back that they were returning and would put on a spectacular final show when they arrived. They alerted the home office because they wanted a good crowd. Ed called, and I put a small announcement in *News Today*. I told the Snooty Skylarks about it. For all my talk about the group, they had never really seen the Gates Flying Circus perform, and this would be their last chance ever. Viola had returned and was there with a guy she was dating named Bill Ulbrich. They all joined me, including Reese, Mother, and Daddy. Wearing a hooded coat, Amelia quietly stepped into our group at the last minute.

Billy Racey and his buddies horsed around nearby. Gerald and Wendell stood off by themselves near the entrance. I smiled and waved, and they returned my greeting.

Word got out, and a crowd of about three hundred people assembled. In addition to average spectators, mechanics of the Wright service hangar and men working in the Fokker factory ran out of the open hangar door.

Notable aviators who happened to be in town at the time huddled in the cold with the rest of us, waiting for the Gates Flying Circus to come home and show off for the last time.

Pang stood by with Judge obediently at his side. Gates drove down from the shops in Lodi and joined him. Early in the afternoon that chilly autumn day, we heard the deep, resonant rumble of the Hisso engines. The weather cooperated. The skies were clear, with only a slight wind. All eyes turned to the southwestern edge of the field. The Standards were still painted red with the Texaco star. Wing to wing, they flew to the middle of the field, a mechanic or stuntman in the front cockpit of each plane. One of them signaled—I think it was Brooks—and they all looped side by side. My guess is that they were at two thousand feet.

I glanced at Pang, who swallowed hard as he watched. Judge barked. Tears welled in Gates's eyes, which he dabbed when he thought no one was looking. Even the toughest on the outside can be sentimental on the inside and let those emotions spill over. This was understandable, considering they were experiencing the swan song of more than a decade of commitment to the organization and the men who flew with them. The respect they had for one another and their camaraderie were unparalleled. Tears glistened in Ed's eyes as well. He made no attempt to hold them back. I could tell he was taking a lot of mental notes.

In all, the aviators performed five side-by-side loops, then broke off in fleur-de-lis and performed their signature tricks. It was then that I could clearly identify which one was Jack. I pointed him out to the others. As I had been in Philadelphia and Endicott, and wherever I had seen Jack fly, I was mesmerized. They ended by each spinning down close to the ground before making a perfect three-point landing. Jack, of course, brought out his bugle and played a little tune before cutting his engine and sideslipping in.

Making up for lost time, I guess, Brooks made one last loop before he landed, the last one down. Then they all taxied to the rail fence at the south end of the field. They flipped back their goggles, cut their switches, and let out a whoop. The crowd joined in, cheering.

The Gates Flying Circus had officially flown its last exhibition. The Gates Flying Circus officially was no more.

SLOWLY, the crowd dissipated, talking quietly and nodding their heads in appreciation.

Daddy was speechless, which didn't happen often. Finally, he spoke. "That was stupendous. Unbelievable. I know I sound like a little kid, but do you think Jack would take me flying sometime?"

"Can I go?" said a quiet voice beside him. It took us several seconds to realize that it came from Mother.

"Uh . . . Look. Pang and Gates have invited us to join them in the back room for a gathering. I'll ask him, okay?"

"Thanks. We'll see you later."

The gathering was in full swing but subdued when we walked in, unlike the raucous party three years before. The guys were talking and smacking the four performers on their backs, congratulating them. I could hear Whispering Bill's voice above everyone else's. Music played on a Victrola, only this time it wasn't so scratchy and loud. I was also reminded that Jack's birthday was coming up. The guys greeted me, Reese, Ruth, and Frances warmly. Viola and Bill stayed a few minutes.

Ed Churchill came over. "Hello, Mavis. I picked up a copy of *News Today* on my way over. You're putting out a fine newspaper, gal."

"Thank you, Ed. I appreciate that. I really do."

"The *Graphic* is what it is and will always be—a tabloid," he said. "I'm doing more freelance writing. Not much for me to do with Gates these days, but there's work around. It's not as much fun, though."

"You've done some good writing for Gates. You kept them in the public eye. I think you were the only paper that covered the attack on New York in '25. I only mentioned it in passing. In fact, I still have the articles you wrote. They are some of my prized pieces of writing."

Ed smiled broadly. "Thanks. Now I'm thanking you. Maybe I'll stop by and see you sometime when I'm on the island."

"I'd like that. What's next for you?"

"There's plenty to write about in New York. New Yorkers like a spectacle, and there's always a spectacle here. Maybe I'll write a book. I've been wanting to do that."

I gave him a look of approval. "I get the first copy."

"Jack can tell a pretty good yarn. I've about convinced him to join the News Writers Association."

"Good idea. I'll bring it up as well."

Jack brought us glasses of champagne on a tray.

"For the ladies and gentlemen," he said with a bow. "Thanks for coming to our little show."

I returned his bow. "Thank you, sir. We wouldn't have missed it for the world. It was breathtaking and a fitting end to the organization. I salute you."

We clinked our glasses.

"Here's to Gates!" Ruth said, and we clinked our glasses.

"Here's to Upside-Down Pangborn and Gates," Brooks roared, and we clinked our glasses.

"Here's to flying," Frances said. And we clinked our glasses.

"Here's to us," I said. And we clinked our glasses.

"Here's to a successful airline," Jack said. And we clinked our glasses.

"Here's to the guy who flew the first woman across the Atlantic," Ed said, nodding to Wilmer Stultz.

"They didn't have to pull her out of the drink like Haldeman and Ruth Elder," someone said to laughter.

"Well, Ruth Elder's taking her 'failure' all the way to the bank and to Hollywood, let me tell you," Ruth said, and everyone laughed again.

"What's next for you, Jack?" Frances asked.

"I don't rightly know. There's one thing I want to do. Did you see those young guys out there? They follow me everywhere. I get a kick out of them. I'm going to teach them to how to work on planes and how to fly for those who want to. Even that Negro feller over by the fence. He's a long shot, but so was I, being born out in the middle of nowhere."

"Good for you," I said.

"Other than that, aviation is changing, so I don't know what's out there or what there will be in the future."

"I know what you mean," Ruth said. "Fairchild has told me that he can't keep me on anymore, so I'm looking for flying work as well."

"Curtiss has asked me to join their exhibition team next year," Frances said.

Jack nodded and held up his glass but looked sympathetic at the same time. "I know it's harder for the gals. I can always settle in here for a while as a mechanic and give flying lessons. People always want a ride. We can put on little shows. Gates found a group of girl acrobats that people like. After the first of the year, me, Bill, and Ive are setting up shop at Holmes, hoping for some commercial work. We're a good team. We'll keep our ears open."

Ruth nodded. "Thanks. That's generous of you."

"You can tell a good story, and I'm sure you have lots of them from the war," I told him. "There's an Association of News Writers. You should join them." I winked at Ed.

"Funny you should say that. Ed just told me the same thing. Maybe I will."

Everyone was talking and having a good time when Pang tapped on his glass to get everyone's attention. "I have permission to announce that Jack has been accepted as an inductee to the society of Quiet Birdmen, and as you know, that's all I can say about that."

Jack looked surprised and honored. Being accepted into the secretive aviation fraternity of the Quiet Birdmen was the envy of any aviator. All I could think of to say was, "Congratulations!" I had so many questions, but there were too many ears around and not enough time.

I changed the subject. "Tonight reminds me of that night when we celebrated your birthday. Remember?"

"Sure do. Seems like a long time ago. Has it only been three years? So much has happened."

"We need to go now, but before I forget, Daddy wanted me to ask you if you would take him for a plane ride and do some stunting. Just mild stuff. He's wanted to do this ever since you took me flying."

"Oh, he has, has he?"

"Yes. Mother says she wants to go too. I think Daddy

can take some stunting, but Mother? No. It's once around the field at fifty feet, and that's it."

They all got a laugh out of that.

"You tell him to be here at two o'clock Sunday afternoon."

Daddy got his stunting flight, and we were there to cheer him on. He was giddy when he climbed out of the plane and for weeks afterwards. He recounted the flight every chance he got at holiday parties to anyone who would listen. Some started avoiding him, so he eased back some.

Mother got her short flight and was very pleased with herself to have accomplished one circuit around the field at an altitude of fifty feet. We were proud of her as well.

The first week in December, Louise Thaden set an altitude record for women in California. Ruth Nichols saw Louise again and told me that she was someone to watch. Ruth Elder was still riding the wave of popularity and making movies in Hollywood. Amelia was writing her memoir of being the first woman to fly across the Atlantic in an airplane. Viola completed a solo endurance flight record for a woman on December 20. Officially, she stayed aloft for eight hours, six minutes, and twenty-seven seconds, but we would have to hear more about it after the first of the year. The purpose of endurance records was for engine manufacturers to prove that their engines were durable for long flights.

I got an engagement ring and set a mid-May wedding date, but then got married on New Year's Day and planned an aerial tour of Africa for April and May.

Happily, we rang in the new year, 1929.

CHAPTER 21
1929

THE SKYLARKS DIDN'T GET TOGETHER until mid-February before Reese and I left. Viola gave us an account of her endurance flight, which was pretty intense hangar flying.

I pounced the minute she walked in. "Okay, Viola. We want to hear all about it. I can't imagine spending hours in a plane just circling."

She laughed. "Well, I borrowed Grace Lyons's plane for the attempt. I got off pretty easily considering I had six hundred pounds of fuel and oil in the front cockpit."

"So, let me stop you there for a moment. The front cockpit was full of fuel, so if you had crashed, the plane could have caught fire, and you would have been charred."

Viola nodded and continued. "There was nothing but blackness all around me. I flew toward Curtiss Field at what I thought was five thousand feet, then switched on the dashboard lights. I was shocked to see that my oil temp was down to zero. My oil pressure was down to one pound per square inch."

Frances looked on in disbelief. "What did you do?"

"The temperature had been sixty when I took off, which was about right. I spent the next couple of minutes trying to remember what Bill had told me to do in such a case. Remember, it was black. Clouds had closed in beneath me. I really didn't know which way was up or down. I know a lot of pilots who've flown at night have had this feeling. Thank goodness I had my altimeter."

"I've heard of that, too, but not experienced it," Ruth said.

"I knew the boys on the field would be really scared for me. I decided to depend on my intuition and said to myself, 'Here goes!' I cut the motor to sixteen hundred revolutions a minute and started toward what I thought was down and back toward Roosevelt Field. I put my confidence in my altimeter and watched it."

"My gosh, Viola. I don't know if I could have kept such a level head. Of course, I wouldn't have had the courage to be up there in the first place," I said. "Please, go on."

"The red beacon at Roosevelt Field appeared when I came out of the clouds. It was the most wonderful sight I ever saw in my life. I was at one thousand feet. I kept it in sight until daylight."

"You can breathe now, Mavis," Frances said, and they all laughed.

"Afterwards, the guys at the field said they were really concerned. They heard the morning gun go off at Mitchel Field, thought I had crashed, and rushed across the field."

"So you made it through the clouds. What then?" Ruth asked.

"I had work to do. I had to pump gas from my spare tank into the gravity tank, where it would flow into the motor. I was so scared and nervous. My fingers shook so that I could hardly work it, but that didn't last long.

"I didn't lose sight of the beacon at Roosevelt. Like I said, I was flying Grace Lyons's ship, and I didn't want to break it up. I was wearing a parachute. They are all right. I believe in them. But mine was very uncomfortable. And I would have stayed with that ship if it had started to burn. She had loaned it to me, and I was going to bring it down the best I could. I christened it the *Grace Lyons* before the flight."

Viola paused for a couple of minutes before continuing.

"After dawn, I kept flying around, keeping the field in sight. At one time, I climbed to two thousand feet, but it got terribly bumpy, so I came back to one thousand.

"All during the night, I was careful to do as I had been told. I kept the nose from getting low and didn't bank too much on right turns. With the heavy load of gas, either one of these might have meant bad news."

I looked at her again in disbelief. "That's just incredible, Viola."

"Was any of the time flying good?" Ruth asked.

She nodded. "The best time was from sunrise until about ten o'clock. Then a mist appeared, and shortly after that it began to rain. I was sorry when the rain dimmed the windshield so I couldn't see anything, and I had to set her down."

Frances got a funny look on her face, like she wanted to ask something but was too embarrassed. Then she blurted out, "What did you do when you had to pee?"

We all burst out laughing, because we all wanted to know.

"Well, you don't drink much before you go up, you only sip water when your mouth gets dry while you're up, and you become a baby again. Modern feminine products help, but the lined flight suit was cumbersome."

Viola went on to tell us that she was considering another endurance flight, but one that involved in-flight fueling. A crew of pilots on the West Coast had set a record in a plane they had named the *Question Mark.*

Jack sent me a short note telling me that he, Ive, and Bill had set up shop at Holmes Airport with Jimmy Scott as their mechanic. He had rented an apartment in Jackson Heights. He was adjusting to domestic life, as he referred to it, but was glad he wasn't selling nuts and bolts in Kansas. Enclosed with the note was a photo of him with Billy and some other boys. Jack was "keeping them out of trouble" by teaching them to be mechanics and showing them how to fly. There was a separate photo of Gerald and Wendell in the front cockpit of a plane with him in the pilot seat. He had to teach Wendell on a separate day. In all, he seemed to be adjusting to his new routine and ready for new adventures.

When Reese and I returned, we settled into a modest home we bought in Great Neck.

Frances and Ruth wanted to meet for coffee on Thursday afternoon, June 27, then go to Roosevelt Field. At Josie's, I asked why they wanted to go to Roosevelt.

"To cheer Jack and Viola on," Frances said.

"Jack and Viola? For what?"

"You've been gone. Of course you wouldn't know. They're attempting an endurance flight. They plan to take off this evening," Ruth said.

"What? That doesn't seem like something Jack would be interested in at all."

"I didn't think so either, but he's doing it," Frances said.

"Let's get over there, then."

At the airfield, Jack and Viola hardly took notice that we were present. Out on the field was a plane with *The Answer* painted on it along with Viola's and Jack's names.

"They say they are going to stay up for over 175 hours or something like that. The *Question Mark* set a record they want to beat. Jack wasn't Viola's first choice. Three other guys dropped out at the last minute for various reasons. Somebody suggested that she talk to Pangborn. He recommended she talk to Jack; he said he's the best. Jack said that he would do it."

"Like I said, I certainly wouldn't have thought that."

"Ruth and I didn't either, but here they are, ready to go. Since he has more experience, Jack's calling the shots. Friends of his will fly the refueling planes from Connecticut twice a day."

"From Connecticut? I wonder why there?"

"I wondered that myself," Frances said, "but I'm not in charge."

"The Jensens and Bill Ulbrich are already up. They will have a rivalry going." She pointed to a plane circling overhead. "That's them. *The Three Musketeers*."

I shook my head at all the news. "All I can say is that I hope all goes well for all of them."

"Get this," Frances said. "People were giving them grief about a man and a woman being alone in an airplane for so long, so they put in a partition behind the cockpit to shut people up."

"You're kidding."

"Nope."

"Let's go check it out."

We peeked inside the cockpit, and sure enough, there it was, behind the seats.

I looked around the interior of *The Answer.* "You know, a closed-cabin plane sure would be nice. I'm going to talk to Daddy about that. I wouldn't like to spend a week in one, but more power to them." We all laughed.

We wished Jack and Viola well and left. They barely noticed that we were there.

That night, I rested well after my busy day, but various airplanes flew in and out of my dreams. Flying around Africa was nice, but it was good to be back home. I snuggled down in bed next to Reese and dreamed of flying in Africa, but suddenly I gasped and sat upright in bed, my heart pounding. I looked at the clock. It read 6:13; I usually arose at seven.

"What is it, love?" Reese asked.

"I don't know if I had a nightmare or what, but I just suddenly woke up very frightened."

"It will be okay," he said. He took me into his arms, and we snuggled and snoozed until seven.

My phone was ringing when I arrived at my office two hours later. "It's been ringing a lot," my secretary said.

Quickly, I unlocked my office and picked up the receiver. "Hello?"

"Mavis. This is Pang. I have bad news."

I sat down. "It's Jack, isn't it?"

"Yes. How did you know? He and Viola crashed this morning. They ran out of gas. The refueling plane couldn't get to them because of fog. Jack was at the controls and was killed instantly. Viola is in pretty bad shape. Her chances are so-so."

I slumped in my chair, my head on my hand. "This is just awful. Jack's such a good fog pilot. Seems like they could have set down okay. It's just flat potato fields out there."

"According to witnesses, they were flying low, preparing to land. They hopped over the water tower at Hicks Nursery. That went okay, but they got too close to that damn hickory tree. The only one for miles. The tail snagged on a branch and brought down the plane. It went straight down. Poor guy didn't have a chance. I'm so sorry. I know you knew them both, but you were really close to Jack. I just talked to Mr. and Mrs. Ashcraft. That was tough."

"I can only imagine," I said. "He had been through so much and was getting his life back together, and now this. Damn."

"I know. I'll have Ed call when we have details about the funeral."

"Thank you, Clyde." I started to hang up. "Oh, Clyde."

"Yes?"

"What time was the crash?"

"The chronometer read 6:1 3."

Immediately, I call Ruth and Frances to tell them the news.

Ed called early that afternoon to tell me Jack's funeral would be Sunday at Campbell's Funeral Chapel. Jack's body would then go to Towanda, Pennsylvania, on its way to its final resting place in Protection, Kansas. Ive and Bill had a plane and were standing by. His mechanic and faithful friend, Jimmy Scott, would be at his side the whole way.

I wanted to talk more, but Ed was too overcome with grief.

CHAPTER 22
THE AVIATION COMMUNITY SAYS GOODBYE

THE TAXI PULLED in front of the chapel. I had told Reese that I preferred to attend the service alone. Gerald and Wendell were standing in the shadows of the entrance of a building close by. When he saw that I was in the car, he instinctively walked over and opened the door for me. He nodded and smiled ever so slightly that he was glad to see me. I returned the sentiment, then motioned for him and Wendell to stand near me. A man with the chapel started to object, but I told him in no uncertain terms that they were with me. He sternly told me they weren't allowed into the main building but had to watch from just inside the exterior doors. I nodded that I understood and pulled a veil over my face.

Somberly, pallbearers waited for the hearse to arrive. I recognized Wilmer Stultz, Bill Brooks, Pangborn, Judge at his side, Warren Smith, and Ivan Gates. Ed was barely holding his emotions together. The others were George Daws and Abraham Greenberg. When the vehicle arrived, they quickly and respectfully removed the wooden box that held Jack's body. Somehow, I held back the tears, for the time being. But then, perhaps I had cried them all.

To make sure Gerald and Wendell would be allowed in, I entered the chapel last. I stood in the entryway and watched while the others filed past his casket. I nodded to Ruth and Frances as they passed. I started forward and wavered. I decided that I wouldn't go to the front. I preferred to remember him that night after the final exhibition of the Gates Flying Circus. Yes, that was how I wanted to remember him. Pulling his life together. Looking forward to the future. Returning to happiness. I could tell that he wore the coveralls that he liked to fly in, which was appropriate, and a newsboy cap—the same attire that he was wearing when I met him at the air races. Ed saved me an aisle seat next to him.

Ruth and Frances looked at me inquiringly. I nodded that I was okay. I appreciated them being there to support me and pay their respects to Jack. Peter Siccaro, chief of police of Bergen County, New Jersey, was there, as was Swanee Taylor. I had seen him at exhibitions. The place was packed to overflowing. People stood in the aisle and against the walls of the chapel.

An article about the service stated that Jack's roommates in Jackson Heights, Hank Doerr and Ive McKinney, had arranged the services. Reverend Doctor Nathan A. Seagle, rector of St. Stephen's Protestant Episcopal Church, would conduct the services.

The Quiet Birdmen, Holmes Airport, Gates Flying Service, and Frank White sent floral tributes. Frank White's was an airplane with a broken wing. There were other beautiful floral arrangements in tribute to Jack. I was amazed at the number of people whose lives he had touched.

From his words, it was obvious the Reverend Doctor had not talked to anyone who knew Jack to write his comments. His words, of which there were too many, were grandiose and were more appropriate for the funeral of a fellow clergyman than a man who had chosen to live in the skies. I heard a jazz band in the distance and thought that Jack would have preferred that the loud group march through the aisles blaring a happy tune on their brass instruments like the ones he used to play on his bugle—a celebration of his life rather than a lament for his death. I believe the Reverend Doctor would have spoken longer, but the eyes of the toughened pilots in the front row bearing down on him persuaded him to do otherwise.

After the service, Ruth and Frances were at my side while the coffin was taken to the hearse and mourners sadly filed out of the chapel and waited for Jack to leave New York for the final time. Gerald and Wendell had already vanished.

I turned to my friends. "Thanks for coming. I appreciate it."

"We liked Jack a lot," Frances said. "Everybody did. He was a brother of the air."

"Skylarks support Skylarks," Ruth added.

"How much?"

Both women looked at me questioningly.

"How much do you support me? I've got to go flying."

Ruth looked at me. "Today? Alone?"

"Yes."

"Are you sure you're up to it?" Frances asked.

"Not a hundred percent, no, but I feel like if I don't fly right away, I'll lose my nerve forever. I've got to prove to myself I can do it. I think Jack would want me to."

"Then we'll be at the field to support you," Frances said.

CHAPTER 23
FLYING FROM FEAR

June 29, 1929, 5:00 p.m., Roosevelt Field, Long Island

OVER THE YEARS, I've observed that pilots are a superstitious lot. They have their talismans, whether it be dice, a rabbit's foot, a photo of a loved one, or even a soft stuffed toy they can tuck into their flight suit. Some won't fly over graveyards. Others drop wreaths on the graves of those who have been killed. Some bless their planes and themselves before takeoff and after landing. Others spit on the tailfin or put chewing gum on a wire before takeoff. None look at the sky for fear that doing so will bring bad weather. Jack threw dust into the wind.

When one of their own is killed, or flies west, they believe they must immediately get back into the cockpit or they will lose their nerve. As unbearable as Jack's funeral was, I knew what I had to do. It was also the last thing I wanted to do—fly. The thought went against all my instincts of self-preservation and sanity. My mind and logic argued with my heart. My mind prevailed. I rushed home, hoping Reese wouldn't be there. Thankfully, he wasn't, or he certainly would have stopped me, or tried to. When he got home and read my note, he would call Daddy, who would call the airport manager, Charles, to tell him to ignore any requests I made concerning flying that day. I rummaged through my closet for my gear. Determined to fly that afternoon, I phoned Charles to tell him to get the Waco ready. I scribbled a note to Reese and, with helmet and goggles in hand, rushed out the door.

Even if I only took off, circled the field, and landed, I knew I had to get back at the controls of an airplane right away. Jack would have wanted me to—would have expected me to.

As I drove to Roosevelt Field, thoughts of Jack, a man I had once loved and still cared for, swirled through my mind. Seeing him laid out, lifeless, in that plain wooden coffin, his skull crushed under the newsboy cap he always wore when he wasn't flying, was the worst day of my life. I'm certain the undertaker had put the cap on him to conceal some damage. The thought was almost too much to bear. I found a piece of chewing gum and began to chew nervously.

At the airfield, the Waco was waiting outside the hangar for me. I immediately started inspecting the plane. Thoughts and remembrances of Jack rolled through my head, interrupting my concentration. I knew that Charles had gone over the aircraft thoroughly and had possibly had someone take it up, but a good pilot checks out her plane. I needed something to do while I conjured the nerve to actually climb into the cockpit. Even though I had flown a lot in recent months, Jack's crash was vivid in my mind. My whole body shook. My hands quivered, but I proceeded as if it was business as usual.

While I was nervous, Jack's courage to get back in the cockpit after Franz and Buck crashed gave me the nerve. I thought of Viola as well, for I believed that she would live and knew she would fly again someday. I thought about her pumping gas in the darkness during her solo endurance flight. Ruth and Frances drove up but stood near their vehicle and observed. I looked their way and nodded that I was okay. They acknowledged my gesture.

Charles watched me carefully as I went about inspecting the plane. He surely noticed my fingers trembling.

"You sure you want to do this?" he asked.

"It's not a matter of wanting to. I have to, or I'll lose my nerve forever."

"Look, what happened to Jack was horrible. Him of all people—and I know you two were close. No one would blame you if you never flew again," Charles said. "Maybe you should wait until next week."

Distracted from my task, I turned and glared at the man I had trusted with my life when he taught me to fly. "Would you have said that to Jack after Franz and Buck were killed?"

Charles looked away and sighed. "Probably not."

"I didn't think so. Jack's dead and Viola is fighting for her life. If she lives, do you think she'll fly again?"

"Probably so. *If* she lives," Charles said quietly, staring at me.

More determined than ever, I completed, then repeated, the flight check. When Charles wasn't looking, I spat on the tailfin and stuck my chewing gum on a wire. I started to climb into the plane, then stooped to get a pinch of moist soil and tossed it into the wind.

As I strapped in, images of *The Answer* at Hicks Nursery with its tail sticking straight up flashed through my mind. Tears welled in my eyes. "For Jack and the others," I whispered. I dried my tears with my scarf and adjusted the goggles over my eyes. After blessing myself, I touched the picture of him that I found in a pocket of my coveralls. Instead of avoiding the sky, I looked up defiantly, daring the weather to stay clear for my flight. I took deep breaths before I started the plane. The engine rumbled to life. Quickly, I taxied down the runway and was soon airborne.

I flew south and circled the Statue of Liberty before heading over Jackson Heights, where Jack had lived. From there, I flew to the city, over Central Park, over Broadway, then northwest to the countryside, but not too far. Apprehension faded as I went about the business of flying. I concentrated on the gauges, stick, and rudders, looking at the ground occasionally in case I had to set down in an emergency. Gradually, the tension went away, and I remembered why Jack had loved flying so much, and why I did. I felt his presence. The air was cooler and sweeter at three thousand feet. My plane was like a little bird flitting high above the treetops, which looked like green fountains under the vast sky. *You're doing fine. You'll be okay*, Jack seemed to whisper.

Reese, Daddy and Mother, and Charles were waiting for me when I landed an hour later. I knew not to push my luck. Ed had joined Frances and Ruth. The plane rolled to a stop, and I alighted from it. Relieved, I hung my head, flipped up my goggles, and victoriously slapped the front of the cockpit.

Removing my flight helmet and shaking my hair, I strode toward the group that waited for me. "Whew! I'm sure glad that's over. I didn't know I would have a welcoming party."

"We were . . . concerned," Reese said.

"You know, Daddy," I said as I walked to where the others were standing, "we need to think about getting a cabin airplane."

"Why?" He laughed. "Reese has one."

Reese gave me a big hug. "Thank goodness you're okay," he said. "You're a good pilot, but . . ."

The others joined us. Daddy looked on, relieved.

I had stopped shaking sometime during the flight, but Reese's arms around me relaxed me further, and I felt calm.

"How was it?" Ruth asked.

"Tense and a little frightening at first, but I concentrated on the business of flying."

Reese held me at arm's length. "I found your note and rushed here as quickly as I could, but I knew that I couldn't stop you if I had wanted to, and in a weird sort of way, I understand."

Ruth and Frances patted me on the back reassuringly.

Daddy nodded, then laughed. "I think I would have chosen more appropriate attire."

I wasn't sure that they couldn't have stopped me, but I would never admit it. And what was done was done.

"I did what I set out to do," I said. "I'm hungry. Let's all go to Josie's."

I took my time getting in to work the next morning. Ed had already been there and left me a note.

Hey, gal. I stopped in to check on you to see how you're doing. I imagine you took Jack's death pretty hard. I sure did. I'm leaving a couple of letters that I wrote when I got home from the funeral. In a way, they were cathartic for me. One is to Mark Hellinger. He said that he will publish it in the New York Daily News. The other is to Jack's dad. Jack talked so much about him that I feel like I know him.

Here's a ticket Pang asked me to give you. He said that you would know what it was about.

I looked at the ticket that I'd found in the newspaper when I first met Jack in Philadelphia and smiled, tears in my eyes. He'd kept it all this time.

Maybe we can get together in a week or so and share the good memories about our friend, Big Jack, Cowboy Aviator.

My Best to You, Ed Churchill

A week later, we did just that.

CHAPTER 24
THINKING BACK

AFTER JACK'S DEATH, I had a different perspective on life and flying. Even though we had drifted apart, and our flight paths had gone in different directions, Jack and his love of life and flying remained a part of me. I hoped they always would. We had loved one another, bonded through our love of aviation, but we became friends as well. Thankfully, Reese understood and gave me time.

No one will ever know the reason for the decisions he made that day, but he must have had no doubt that his friend would come through. The camaraderie and bond between aviators is that strong. I now feel a similar bond with Ruth, Frances, Viola, and other women pilots who fly through Roosevelt and Curtiss Fields. This was something I didn't expect. Ruth had trusted me that day we flew back from Virginia, and we made it. My confidence as a pilot grew. I loved our group. To me, we weren't the least bit snooty. We just needed others like us to talk to. We understood one another. All the while, I knew our paths would drift apart.

The fliers of the World's Greatest Exhibition Aviators

drifted their own ways but remained in aviation-related enterprises. Some were killed, like Stultz, who met death less than a week after Jack crashed.

By some miracle and pure pluck, Viola survived the crash. When we were allowed to visit her months later, she said that she asked Jack twice if he wanted to land when the fog rolled in. She said they could fly another day. He said no both times. He told her that he would land if she wanted to, but if they did, she would have to get another pilot, because he had things he wanted to do. That said, she wasn't going to ask again, and she buckled in as he told her to do. She wanted a good record as well. Sometimes, you just have to be courageous when the outcome is unknown. As it turned out, that silly partition probably saved her life. In all, she spent eighteen months in the hospital.

From our conversations while recovering, I knew that she would fly again.

I continued to report the news. Readership was good. Subscriptions for the paper continued to increase. Advertising paid the bills and more. A lot more.

Frances and Ruth were excellent pilots, but finding consistent work flying was a challenge. However, they persisted and flew when they could. Frances was on the Curtiss exhibition team and participated in races. She was good at them. Ruth made an unsuccessful attempt to cross the Atlantic.

In August of 1929, an all-women's air derby opened the Cleveland National Air Races. This was a breakthrough for women pilots. Will Rogers dubbed it the "Powder Puff Derby." He was supportive but observed the women powdering their noses before they got into their planes. Ruth, Frances, and Amelia all participated. In all, twenty women participated in two classes of airplanes. Louise Thaden and Phoebe Omlie won.

In November, with Amelia, Ruth Nichols, and Louise leading the way, women pilots formed the Ninety-Nines International Organization of Women Pilots. Accompanied by a nurse, Viola was allowed to attend the first meeting of the organization in Valley Stream, New York, and was a founding member. The Snooty Skylarks continued to meet for a time, but the group eventually dissolved as we each went our own ways.

I waffled for a time about getting my license and continuing to fly, then asked myself, why would I stop? I could think of no instance when the crash of a fellow pilot had deterred someone from flying. I knew Reese would support me. He already had. There were several husband/wife teams flying, like Louise and Herbert Thaden. Frances married her instructor. There was also Hazel and Ivan Gates. Reese and I could share experiences flying that people bound to the earth could only dream about. I thought of the vacations we could have while avoiding traffic snarls. If we had children, we would bring them along. The people I hired could run the paper in my absence. My basic license renewed, I concentrated on honing my skills toward a transport license.

The stock market crashed in October of 1929, and with that came uncertainty, but I was confident aviation would move forward.

In faster, more nimble and reliable planes, men and women pilots would race and break records. Endurance times in the air would be smashed. Aviators would cross the Atlantic Ocean many times in both directions. On the West Coast, flights to Hawaii would be more frequent. Amelia was one pilot who flew across the Pacific. In short, aviators would fly higher, faster, and longer. As Pangborn had told Jack several years before, I must be prepared to lose more friends.

I attended that first meeting of the Ninety-Nines but chose not to become a member. While I certainly support women who fly, I don't consider myself a professional pilot. I fly recreationally. With Reese's guidance, I constantly improve my skills, and we have had some fabulous excursions.

Before I knew it, a year had passed since Jack's death. Over Labor Day, Pangborn and a couple of flying buddies flew to Jack's hometown and dropped wreaths on Jack's grave and that of his brother, Franz. He brought copies of the articles about the event to Ed and me.

Mr. and Mrs. Ashcraft placed a full sheet on Jack's grave and a sheet on the lower half of Franz's grave. I visualized the three planes flying, probably north to south, as one of the pilots swooped low to drop a wreath on Franz's grave. They then circled, and Pang swooped low to drop the second wreath on Jack's grave before flying back to the airport in Dodge City. What a wonderful tribute to a fallen comrade. Pangborn then had lunch with the family and a few friends in the home of Jack's sister.

The last two paragraphs of the article gave me pause:

And thus goes the world. Just a brief pause, just a tear now and then, just a fleeting moment from the busy cares of the present, just a word or two of regret for the fallen comrades so bravely sacrificed and for the friend whose untimely fate cut short such promising lives. But such is life. It is the now that calls. Sorrow must be suppressed. Regrets laid aside as vain. It is the now, the present that calls. Action, living is kind and demands all.

But it is a fine thing to take this pause, to drop a tear, to give a thought now and then to loved ones gone on whose presence we miss and whose going has left an ever-increasing void.

Pang told me Jack's grave marker said "Brief, brave and glorious was his young career." When asked, that's what I had told them that I would put on it.

I UNLOCKED MY OFFICE. Waiting for me on my desk was a package from Ed. Eagerly, I opened it, withdrew a book, and smiled, tears in my eyes. The title of the book was *The Cowboy Aviator and the Lady* by Edward Churchill. Inside was a note.

Hey, gal. It took me awhile, but I got it done. You said if I ever wrote a book, you got the first copy, so here it is. I hope you're not offended by the title, but I was always fascinated with your relationship with Jack. Maybe I was a little jealous, too. And no matter how I tried, I couldn't have him die the way he did. He was too brave and glorious for that. I imagined a life if he had lived. And after all, it is fiction. Best, Ed Churchill.

The End

In 2024, I published *Big Jack, Cowboy Aviator*, a biographical novel about my great uncle John Wesley "Jack" Ashcraft Jr., who was a pilot with the Gates Flying Circus in the 1920s. Readers told me that they liked the fictional character Mavis in the story. Mavis was also a pilot, so I wrote a sequel to my novel from Mavis's point of view and included female pilots of the day. This is a work of historical fiction, with true events intermixed with events from my imagination.

Unfortunately, most women fliers of the 1920s didn't leave personal accounts of their experiences. For most, there is little information readily available. Flying, dialogue, and other events with Mavis are fictional. The Snooty Skylarks are fictional. However, Frances Harrell did fly with the Curtiss Exhibition Team and participated in races in the 1930s. Ruth Nichols was an accomplished aviator and accompanied a young woman to Europe, where they traveled by plane. She set a speed record from New York to Miami in a seaplane, was hired by the Fairchild Airplane Manufacturing Corporation, and set up aviation clubs throughout the United States. Nichols also planned a solo flight across the Atlantic with the assistance of Clarence Chamberlin, but the flight was not to be.

Viola Gentry described some of her experiences in her book *Hangar Flying*. The collection includes her recollections of the attempted endurance flight with Jack, which I paraphrased. The book is an anthology of stories of early aviators that she gathered as consultant for the History of Aviation Collection at the University of Texas at Austin and University of Texas at Dallas. Jennifer Bower has written a nice biography of Gentry titled *North Carolina Aviatrix Viola Gentry: The Flying Cashier*.

Though not as many, there were women pilots at the time, and they were good. I first learned of them researching my uncle and have since become reacquainted with them. In some ways, I feel as if I know them. Although she was an accomplished pilot in her own right, I believe they have been overshadowed by Amelia Earhart's fame.

There were notable pilots before them, and many after them during the late 1920s and 1930s, considered the Golden Age of Flight, and beyond. Though there had been National Air Races since 1919, it wasn't until 1929 that women were allowed to participate. In 1929, the Women's Air Derby from Santa Monica to Cleveland, Ohio, opened the Cleveland National Air Races. Humorist Will Rogers noticed the women touching up their makeup before taking off, so he dubbed the race the Powder Puff Derby. The name has persisted to this day. The prize was $25,000. In heavy and light plane classes, twenty pilots participated:

Florence "Pancho" Lowe Barnes

Marvel Crosson*

Amelia Earhart

Ruth Elder
Claire Mae Fahy
Edith Foltz
Mary Haizlip
Jessie Miller (Australian)
Opal Kunz
Mary von Mach
Ruth Nichols
Blanche W. Noyes
Gladys O'Donnell
Phoebe Omlie
Neva Paris
Margaret Perry
Thea Rasche (German)
Louise Thaden
Evelyn "Bobbi" Trout
Vera Dawn Walker

Louise Thaden won the heavy plane class.
Phoebe Omlie won the light plane class.

*Marvel Crosson was killed during the race.

Before these ladies were pioneer aviators Harriet Quimby, who flew across the English Channel in 1912, and Matilde Moisant. Blanche Stuart Scott learned to fly in 1910 under the tutelage of Glenn Curtiss. In 1915, flying a pusher airplane, Ruth Bancroft Law performed two loops at Daytona Beach. In 1916, she set a cross-country speed record flying from Chicago to New York state, a total of 592 miles. Katherine Stinson became the youngest licensed female aviator in 1912. She was a skywriter and the first woman to fly at night. Her sister Marjorie Stinson earned her license in 1914. With their brother, Eddie, they started a flying school in Texas and taught Canadian cadets to fly during World War I. When flying schools refused to accept Bessie Coleman, the first African American woman to earn her license, she learned French and traveled to France. On June 15, 1925, she became the first Black woman to earn her pilot's license.

After the Women's Air Derby, Gladys O'Donnell formed a club of the women who participated in the race and named them the Skylarks. As a shout-out to Gladys and the Ninety-Nines, I named Mavis's group the Snooty Skylarks. In November of 1929, a more formal group was formed. Their first meeting was in Valley Stream, New York. The group decided on the name the Ninety-Nines, Inc., International Organization of Women Pilots for the number of licensed women pilots at the time. The organization remains active today. Viola Gentry, Ruth Nichols, Amelia Earhart, Ruth Elder, and Louise Thaden were founding members. Gentry was allowed to attend the meeting but was accompanied by a nurse.

To continue the tradition of the first 1929 Women's Air Derby, the Ninety-Nines hosts the Air Race Classic each year. In 2024, I volunteered to help with the race on their stopover in Bartlesville, Oklahoma. Seeing these amazing young women doing their flybys, landings, plane inspections, and takeoffs, the seeds of *Mavis Perkins, Flying Journalist* began to take root. Meeting them in the terminal and listening to them, I knew I had to write a book with female pilots. They would be the same age. Of special interest to me was the warm camaraderie that the older pilots shared with one another. It was a tremendous experience.

My fascination with women pilots and men pilots of the 1920s continues. If you have information about any mentioned in my books or others, I encourage you to contact me through my website: CindyWeigand.com.

I hope to learn more names of earlier aviators and possibly have a website devoted to these early aviators, men and women.

ACKNOWLEDGMENTS

As always, thanks to my family for their support, and to my readers Julia Lauria Blum and Jennifer Bean Bower. Julia is a fellow enthusiast of aviation history and has been a supporter for twenty-five years. As before, Aaron Redfern with Historical Editorial was most helpful and efficient as was JennyQ.

Through the years, the Cradle of Aviation Museum on Long Island has been particularly helpful, so I send a special thank-you to them.

CAVU,
Cindy

FOR MORE INFORMATION

BOOKS

Adams, Jean, and Margaret Kimball, in Collaboration with Jeanette Eaton. *Heroines of the Sky*. Garden City, NY: Doubleday, Doran and Company, 1942.

Bower, Jennifer Bean. *North Carolina Aviatrix Viola Gentry: The Flying Cashier*. Charleston, SC: The History Press, 2015.

Gentry, Viola. *Hangar Flying*. Chelmsford, MA: Privately published, 1975.

Jessen, Gene Nora. *The Powder Puff Derby of 1929: The First All-Women's Transcontinental Air Race*. Naperville, IL: Sourcebooks, Inc., 2002.

Mitchell, Charles R. and Kirk W. House. *Flying High: Pioneer Women in American Aviation*, Images of Aviation. Charleston, SC: Arcadia Publishing, 2002.

Notaro, Laurie. *Crossing the Horizon, A Novel*. New York, NY: Gallery Books, 2016.

O'Brien, Keith. *Fly Girls: How Five Daring Women Defied*

All Odds and Made Aviation History. Boston, MA: Houghton Mifflin Harcourt, 2018.

Thaden, Louise. *High, Wide, and Frightened*. New York, NY: Stackpole Sons, 1938.

Weigand, Cindy. *Big Jack, Cowboy Aviator, A Novel*. Tulsa, OK: Privately published, 2024.

DOCUMENTARIES AND VIDEOS

https://www.youtube.com/watch?v=IAi_AaEQpOw&t=65s
https://breakingthroughtheclouds.com/
https://www.youtube.com/watch?v=rgatVzTDPZo
https://www.youtube.com/watch?v=9F8Ss1FVNPA
https://www.youtube.com/watch?v=tzaro2XIUJo&t=11s

WEBSITES

International Women's Air and Space Museum
https://iwasm.org/wp-blog/

The Ninety-Nines
https://www.ninety-nines.org/who-we-are.htm
https://www.airraceclassic.org/

www.ingramcontent.com/pod-product-compliance
Lightning Source LLC
Chambersburg PA
CBHW060317310726
48976CB00007B/2360